D

This book is dedicated to all the ones we've loved and lost.

They may be gone, but they live on through us.

Copyright

"Honey, it's already been an hour," she replied. "They need to move her."

My eyes followed hers towards the door, where a man and a woman stood just on the other side of the frame.

"An hour?" I asked, turning my attention back to her. My brows furrowed as I gripped Natalie's hand in mine. It was only slightly colder than I remembered. She always had bad circulation. But it had gotten worse in the last few months.

"Leo—" she said again.

I nodded. "Ah—two more minutes?" I asked, my eyes drifting back to Natalie.

I don't know if Theresa responded, but I took her hand squeezing my shoulder as the go-ahead to spend two more minutes in the room with my wife.

Natalie's hair wasn't as shiny and vibrant as it had been for the entire time I had known her. Her skin was dry. Her body was frail. Her eyes were sunken.

"I didn't want you to see me like that."

I glanced around when hearing Natalie's voice. But she wasn't there. Just the memory of her was.

I shut my eyes. Feeling her closeness from a moment we had shared the past summer.

"I want you to remember me as I am," Natalie said, snuggling up against my chest as I held her in my arms.

"A pain in my ass?" I asked with a chuckle.

"Yes, the biggest."

Chapter One
{Saturday, September 23ʳᵈ, 2017}

My hand was on hers.

It didn't move. It didn't flinch. There was no shock that was felt through the earth, let alone her body. Nothing happened.

No long-drawn-out beep that you hear in movies. No indication that death had arrived. Well, except the fact that her chest no longer rose and fell in a slow shallow rhythm.

"Leo—" I heard from beside me. But the tone was low, barely audible, or maybe it was because I was listening intently for one sound. Hoping I was wrong and that I would hear Natalie's breathing start again.

"Leo," I heard once more.

My eyes drifted from my wife's lifeless body up to her mother's eyes.

She was crying. Of course she was crying. She had just lost her daughter.

"Leo, you need to get up," she said, her voice sounding sweeter and softer than I had ever heard her speak.

It wasn't that she was a loud woman. Just that she knew how to use her voice to get a point across.

"Um—" I tried to begin but needed to clear my throat. "I'd like to just sit with her for a few more minutes."

Her eyes looked weary. I didn't want her to have to comfort me. I should have been comforting her.

Content Warnings

Also on:

www.JenniferJensenBooks.com

I blinked as the tears fell from my eyelashes down my cheeks. My calloused hands rubbed against my face, more aggressively than I was certain was needed to wipe them away.

I took a deep breath and rose to my feet, seeing orange as my vision took a moment to return to normal. Looking at Natalie's face one more time before the vultures came to take her.

"That's not nice."

I could hear her voice in the air around me.

I grinned just slightly at her judgmental tone, before I lowered myself to her head. I brushed the top of it with the back of my fingers as I leaned in to kiss her forehead.

"I love you," I whispered as one of my tears dripped onto her cheek and rolled down it.

The floorboards creaked behind me.

My two minutes were up.

Her life was up.

And now, so was mine.

I walked out of the room, passing the scavengers and the family members that had been staying in my house for the past two weeks, waiting for that day to come.

I didn't make eye contact with any of them. I didn't want to look at their need to be comforted and not be able to.

I was their source of comfort. I was everyone's rock. I didn't know how to be the weak one.

The door to the garage slammed behind me as I eyed my tool bench. A project that I had started a year before sat front and center.

The tools I had been using lay beside it. The entire display collecting dust.

"Hey, you ready to go?" Natalie asked.

I set down my hammer and glanced over at her.

"Yeah, two more minutes," I replied, making a mark with my pencil and placing it back behind my ear.

"Ya know, this whole construction thing really works for you," she continued, leaning her back against my bench.

"Yeah?" I responded as I shifted my focus to her.

I looked down at her black boots with matching leggings extending up from them. Her long forest green sweater went mid-thigh, hugging her in all the right places.

"Oh no," she said, causing my eyes to meet hers.

"Oh no, what?" I asked.

"You got that look in your eye, and we don't have time for that."

I rolled my eyes exasperatedly and then smiled. "Hey, you came on to me. Don't be coming at me with that carpenter fantasy shit if you're not going to let me fuck you on my tool bench."

"Leo Algar," she laughed, playfully offended. "I will act out all fantasies with you, but it will have to be after my appointment."

My smile fell just a little, but the shift in the room was felt by us both.

Her expression softened as she reached for my hand and then squeezed it. "Hey, everything's going to be okay. This is where they tell us everything is fine and that we worried for nothing."

I gave her my best reassuring smile and tugged at her hand so that her green sweater was pressed tightly against my red flannel. My lips met hers as I savored the tingle of her Burt's Bees Chapstick that came with every kiss she gave.

I blew on the tools, seeing the dust rush into the air, and then settle moments later. The birdhouse I had been working on to add to our landscaped yard was still in separate pieces, but really only about four steps away from being completed.

"So, Doc, give it to us straight. Is whatever's going on with me from Lydia?" Natalie asked.

Lydia was what Natalie and I called her lupus. She found it comforting to refer to Lydia as a person. That way when we were pissed at Lydia for ruining our night, or our plans in general, it felt like we had a real person to be mad at, and not just her own body.

The doctor smiled briefly at Natalie's lighthearted way of speaking of Lydia, but the expression that came next made my entire body tense up. Then I felt Natalie's do the same.

"Come on, Peter," Natalie said to him, her voice doing everything it could not to shake. "What's Lydia gotten us into this time?"

"I'm afraid she isn't to blame for this one. At least, not as far as we can tell."

My body shifted to the front of the chair. For some reason I must have known that it would be edge of your seat type news. And I was right.

"Natalie—" he cleared his throat. *"You have what is called glioblastoma—"*

The wood from the birdhouse I had never gotten around to finishing was still rough in spots from the partial sanding job I had done. I ran my thumb across it, picturing Natalie's green sweater, black leggings and matching boots.

Glen had come to finish what Lydia had started. Glen was much faster and more powerful than Lydia. And we had spent so much time battling her, that we didn't even think to watch out for him.

I sighed, putting the wood back down on the bench, and picked up my hammer. Now was as good a time as any to start cleaning, right?

I had put reality on hold that day. We had left our normal life behind to live out her days how she wanted to. That meant old projects would be left to collect dust. Because what was the need for birdhouses if the woman I had been building them for wasn't around to use them?

My grip tightened around the handle of the hammer as my eyes seared into the roof of the birdhouse. It was a piece I had glued and held together while Natalie had told me the colors she had picked out for each one.

The tears that had dried during my walk to the garage threatened to resurface as I tried with everything in me to hold them back. But as I concentrated on doing that, I felt my arm lift and without warning, I heard the sound of a hammer on wood.

The roof split into pieces as the glue was no match for steel. I found myself unable to stop the destruction.

I threw my arms onto my bench and whipped them to the side, sending all its contents across the garage and to the floor. I pulled everything off of the shelving and chucked it as far as I could in the other direction until the ground was covered and nothing was left in its place.

"I'm not going to be able to help clean this up," Natalie's voice said, freezing my body amidst the chaos-filled room.

I exhaled.

"You wouldn't have, even if you were still here," I answered back with a small chuckle.

Talking to myself seemed absurd, but the feeling I got when responding to one of her witty remarks made me feel less alone.

***

"Leo."

I pulled at the collar of my suit. Why the fuck was I wearing a suit?

"'Cause you promised me you would."

I smiled at the sound of Natalie's voice.

"Leo."

Maybe I needed to loosen my tie. God, I hated that stupid long piece of fabric. Maybe it was because I always sucked at putting them on. Maybe I should have gotten my mom to help me.

"Maybe you should have learned to do it yourself instead of having me do it for you."

I smiled again. Natalie was right. I should have learned. But after that day, I had zero plans of wearing a tie ever again.

"Leo," I heard as a hand gripped my shoulder, startling me. "Sorry, man," Ethan said as he took a seat next to me. "Everyone cleared out into the banquet room. Did you want to walk with me or stay here?"

I glanced at him, only catching part of what he had said.

I gave a light smile. "I just need two more minutes."

He nodded but didn't get up. Instead he clasped his hands together in his lap and stared up at Natalie's casket.

It was closed. She had requested that. I had thought I would be upset about it once the day had arrived. But now I didn't know how I would've handled it any other way. The large picture of her from two years ago sitting next to all the flowers was hard enough. If I saw her body, I didn't know what I would do.

I stood up. Ethan probably thought it was to exit the room. But really it was to get a better look at the few pictures put together in a frame—more than likely—by her mom.

I ran my finger over her senior picture, and let it trail down to the one below it. The one of us the year we started dating. Our junior year of high school.

"This is the syllabus for the semester. These are the books we will be reading. If you have already read them, then may I suggest reading them again. There are always new things to get out of old books."

I took the paper from Mr. Larson and turned it over to the reading list.

I had read four of the five we were expected to read that semester. The class was going to be a cakewalk.

"What if we've already read the books multiple times?" I heard a girl ask from the back of the classroom.

Mr. Larson turned around to look at her. "Well, then, you will probably have no trouble with the assignments."

"Don't you have a reading list that's a little more challenging?" she asked.

That time many more eyes went to her, mine included.

She didn't glance around at anyone. She just kept her focus on Mr. Larson, waiting for his answer.

But while everyone else seemed to turn their attention back to the syllabus, I didn't.

Her wardrobe screamed "I was pried from my bed with two minutes to find clothes and run out the door." Her hair was surprisingly neat, compared to the amount of wrinkles in her clothing. I wasn't sure if she had been going for the disheveled look, but even if she wasn't, she wore it incredibly well.

Her eyes met mine, I had realized I had been staring long enough to be caught. Even worse, I hadn't realized Mr. Larson had not only answered her question but moved on.

"Mr. Algar, your eyes are better suited at the front of the classroom," I heard Mr. Larson say. That made her smile.

I smiled too, just before Mr. Larson called me out in front of the class once more.

"Hey, man," I heard as a hand hit gently between my shoulder blades, and then stayed there for a moment until I turned my head.

"Hey, Mark," I replied, avoiding eye contacts. "Thanks for coming."

"Of course. You know I'm always here for you."

He said it like it was a fact. But that hadn't been true in years. He was there because my wife was dead. Everyone was. And no matter what any of my friendships or former friendships had been left like, they were all there to show their support.

"Beth's here, too," he continued. "She's with the group."

"The group?" I asked, furrowing my brows, looking once more at Natalie's pictures.

"In the luncheon area. It's like a damn college reunion in there," he said with an odd amount of fondness. He must have forgotten we were standing next to my wife's casket and not a keg or a bonfire. "Nat would have loved to have the group together again."

My eyes met his. But it was brief. I held back an eye roll.

Who was he to say what Natalie would have liked? He and Beth hadn't talked to us in years. An almost decade-long friendship seemingly gone overnight.

"Everyone would really like to talk to you," he said as I glanced over to see Ethan still sitting in the chair, hands clasped together, waiting for me to exit as well.

I nodded and pulled at my collar.

"Just get through the luncheon and then you never have to wear one again."

I sighed, hoping that what Natalie had said was true.

***

"I mean, Jesus, I'm thirty-two next month. I can't even imagine that just being it, ya know?"

That was the line that welcomed me into the banquet room. It shouldn't have surprised me that it was said by Beth. She was known for her woe-is-me mentality.

"Leo—" she said, her expression changing to heartache as her arms flew around me.

"Hi, Beth," I said, doing little to return the embrace.

"I'm so sorry about Natalie. She was such an incredible woman."

So incredible yet she abandoned their friendship?

"Be nice."

Natalie's voice had a bite to it even in the afterlife. I wanted to smile at it, but I didn't want Beth to think she was the one who had made me smile.

"She was," I finally answered.

"If you need anything, Mark and I are just a phone call away."

I scoffed at that. But I made it seem like I was clearing my throat instead.

Beth returned to her spot in the circle as I glanced around at the large turnout of people who had come to pay their respects to my wife. I knew I should mingle, say thank you to each of them for coming. But talking in general wasn't high on my to-do list, so I stayed surrounded by former friends as Mark and Ethan joined the group.

I glanced at Mark. He looked the same, although he had a few more crease lines on his face than when we had first met.

"Dibs on the bed by the window," a guy shouted as he rushed past me.

I raised my brow, annoyed that I had left my house where I shared a room with my little brother, to now share one with a stranger.

The guy threw his stuff on the mattress and looked up at me like he had just won a trophy. And maybe he had.

"Sorry, hope that's cool," he said, his expression wanting to be apologetic, but not quite getting there.

"I don't care," I replied.

It wasn't like I planned on being there all that much. I wanted to be wherever Natalie was. And the fact that I was away from my parents' house and still unable to have her with me was torture. Even worse that she was on the same campus but unable to share buildings.

"Leo, where you at?" my dad hollered.

"On the left," I replied as I set my two suitcases down by the bed adjacent to the window.

"Not too shabby," my dad said as he set everything down in the doorway, as if the weight of my stuff would have been too much to walk even two more feet with.

I picked it up off the floor and put it on my bed.

12

My dad stepped over what was left, approached the other guy in the room, and stuck out his hand.

"My kid's got no manners. I'm Roger."

The trophy holder shook his hand. "I'm Mark."

"This is Leo, if he failed to mention that."

Mark chuckled. "He had failed to mention that."

"Your mom's guarding the car. We should probably get back down," my dad said with a smile.

I nodded and shifted the rest of the stuff out of the doorway.

Mark walked with us down the three flights of stairs. He was parked next to us, although he was kind enough to park slightly on the sidewalk.

"This is Mark, Leo's roommate," my dad said to my mom, as Mark opened his trunk.

He glanced over at them, and then straightened up and walked over to shake her hand.

"I'm Rita," she said, taking his hand in hers.

I jumped as I was poked in the side.

I heard a giggle, and then turned and saw Natalie.

She had ridden with her mom and knowing Theresa and her ability to be perpetually late, they had probably just arrived.

"Is this your sister?" Mark asked, turning towards us.

I put my arm around Natalie's waist.

"Nope, girlfriend," she answered. "And you are?"

"Bummed," he stated as I raised my brow. "Just kiddin' man," *he added, hitting my shoulder like I was the one he needed to* *apologize to. "I'm Leo's roomie," he finally answered.*

Natalie didn't seem overly impressed, but she extended her hand *and gave her usual gorgeous smile.*

"Shit," I heard someone say, just before glass shattered against the ground.

I, along with the group, looked over to the noise.

Diane exhaled as she knelt down to pick up the shards of glass. She looked to be scolding herself under her breath.

"Guess someone's still a little high-strung," Beth said, gritting her teeth.

I contained another eye roll and walked over to Diane as she stood.

"Sorry, Leo, I didn't mean to make a scene."

"I don't think anyone even noticed," I lied.

"I was just trying to get some things cleaned up."

"You don't have to do that. We paid for the clean-up service."

Her eyes met mine. "I just need to keep busy," she added, giving me a forced smile.

"How are you holding up?" I asked as we walked to the garbage.

"Pretty sure I'm supposed to be asking *you* that. *You're* the husband."

"*You're* the best friend," I retorted.

The remnants of the glass fell into the bag, and Diane sighed once more. "Honestly—" she began. "Not great. I keep going to call her and then, like two rings in, I realize she isn't going to answer."

I chuckled, but there was no life in it. "So you're the reason her phone keeps going off."

"You didn't check that it was me?"

I shook my head, but only briefly as another round of grief struck. "I haven't gone back into our room yet, and that's where it's at. It's still on the charger."

"Shit, it definitely has one helluva charge by now."

That time my smile was real; hers was too. But it wouldn't last, and a few seconds later, we were right back where we started.

"I'm going to go check the trays and make sure they are keeping them full," she said.

"I'm just going to reiterate—we are paying someone to handle that. You can just hang out."

She playfully slapped my arm. "You know the only way I thrive is by controlling the situation."

"Well, then, control away."

"—I follow the rules, especially pertaining to quiet hours—" Natalie's roommate Diane said to her as she sat on her bed, and I stood in the doorway of their dorm.

"Quiet hours?" I asked.

Both girls shot me a look.

"Did you not read the information given to you about your room?" Diane asked, furrowing her brow.

"I skimmed it," I replied with a shrug.

"Okay," she replied with an exhale. "Well quiet hours are Monday through—"

"—I read them," Natalie stated, clearly trying her best to remain calm at the lecture a girl her own age was giving her. "I'm not a very loud person, and I love my sleep, so I'm sure it will be no issue."

"And overnight guests are only permitted six days a semester," she continued, seeming to address me more than anyone.

"So no sex during quiet hours and only all-night-marathon-sex six times a semester. Got it," I said with a grin.

Diane's expression didn't change, and Natalie tried to contain her laughter.

"Joke all you want," Diane stated. "But I'm here for two years to get my basic law education out of the way, and then I'm Stanford-bound. That means lots of studying for me. So if you don't get in my way, I won't get in yours."

"Leo," Diane said, her eyes narrowing at mine.

"Yeah?"

Her expression remained questionable. "You seem kind of out of it. Have you eaten anything?"

I smirked. "You think my mom's letting me starve?"

She shook her head and crossed her arms. "Where is Rita?"

"Probably in the kitchen helping them cook," I joked. "You and my mom seem to be cut from the same cloth."

She slapped my arm once more.

16

"I mean that in the best way possible," I added.

Her eyes scanned over the crowd of people as mine followed suit.

They were all eating, catching up—laughing even.

But I wasn't angry with them.

To them, today was just another day. Maybe a slightly sadder one, but their lives hadn't changed from Natalie's absence. Many of them were co-workers or old friends, people that had come in and out of our lives but weren't a constant.

Outside of Diane and our immediate family, no one else was suffering. At least not the same soul-crushing heartache we were feeling from her absence.

***

When we arrived home from the funeral, I pulled at my tie until it was loosely hanging from my neck. I waited for my mom and dad to come in, then Teresa, before I shut the door to my house.

"I'll be taking off in the morning," Teresa said, her eyes avoiding mine. But maybe I was just reading more into it than there was.

"Yeah, Roger has to be back to work Monday morning," my mom chimed in. "So we will be taking off sometime tomorrow, too."

I assumed from my mother's tone that saying so was her way of giving me a heads-up, without having to directly tell me. I could sense she was nervous to leave. She had been making every meal for me for the past three weeks. She was more than likely terrified that her son was going to starve. And maybe I would.

My parents had both come to stay when hospice said Natalie only had a few days left. But like the fighter Natalie was, she hung on a bit longer than they had anticipated. I had a sneaking suspicion that it was more for me than for her. But she wasn't able to talk at the end—only look at me and listen. And while I was telling her she could go. I was certain my eyes were sending an entirely different message.

"Goodnight, Leo," Teresa said, leaning in to kiss me on the cheek. "Try and get some sleep," she continued with a soft smile.

I nodded, forcing a similar expression back.

"Good night, baby," Mom said, following Teresa's kiss with one of her own.

My dad followed that up with an almost uncomfortably awkward hit to the upper arm.

They went to their respective guest rooms as I stood barely inside my front door, shoes still on, with my tie dangling over my chest.

I thought about going for a walk. Our housing development was quiet. I could get some air—some exercise.

I sighed. I didn't have the energy for anything.

"Get some sleep."

Natalie's voice, while always welcomed, hit hard in that moment.

But before the tears broke the surface, my mouth salivated as my stomach did a somersault that rolled through my chest.

I ran down the hall, barely making it to the toilet before the little I had eaten at the funeral resurfaced, acid and all.

Once the heaving stopped, I pushed the handle down and flushed the toilet.

The sound of the lid slamming shut echoed off the walls as I leaned back against the edge of the tub and extended my legs out in front of me.

I looked down at my tie. Somewhere in the mix of revisiting my meal, it had gotten in the way.

Grabbing a hold of it from behind my neck, I pulled it off and threw it across the bathroom with a lackluster effort.

"Get some sleep."

"I can't," I told her. "I need you here so I can sleep again."

When she didn't respond, I shut my eyes, trying to keep the burning sensation at bay. It helped with the physical pain, but closing my eyes only gave me room to experience another round of the emotional kind.

"I'm Leo," I said confidently as I approached the beautifully disheveled girl after class.

"I'm Natalie," she responded, her lips curling slightly.

"Did you just move here?"

"Yeah, last week," she replied.

"Where from?"

"Ventura, California."

She grabbed her papers and we walked towards the hall.

"Oh, wow. So what brought you to Oregon?" I asked.

"My mom's from here," she replied. "So when my dad left us to run off with his secretary, we didn't really have a choice."

My eyes widened.

"I'm kidding," she responded with a grin.

I laughed, although it was kind of awkward. I was nervous for a second because I wouldn't have known what to say.

"It wasn't his secretary. It was just some woman he met at a bar, but that sounds less classy."

She looked at me to gauge my reaction. I had no idea what expression I was sporting.

"Sorry," she continued. "I'm still navigating this whole talking to other humans thing since it happened."

"Totally understandable," I replied. "So you've read the entire list of books multiple times?"

I could tell she appreciated the change in subject. "Yeah, Pride and Prejudice *is my favorite."*

We arrived at what I assumed was her locker. She leaned up against it and looked up at me.

"I enjoyed it too," I replied.

She raised her brow. "You're a Jane Austin fan?"

"I don't know if I would say fan," *I replied with a shrug. "I enjoyed the book, but it's probably just a one-time read for me."*

"Yeah? What's a multiple-times read for you?" she asked, opening her locker.

"I've read Tuesdays with Morrie *probably ten times since it came out."*

That piqued her interest. "Really? I've heard good things. It's on my list of want-to-reads."

"Well, maybe if you stopped reading Jane Austin, you could read other books."

"That'll never happen."

I chuckled. "You're going to miss out on some great books."

"Nah, I'll get around to them; it just might take me a little longer."

The bell rang, causing me to jump.

She laughed.

"We should probably get to class," I said.

"Or we could just skip and go read on the football field."

Intrigued, I raised my brows.

"I'm kidding," she replied with a grin. "We can save that for a later in the year event."

"Oh? An event?"

She shrugged. "We can make it one."

"The bell has rung!" one of the teachers said as she grabbed the knob on the door she was closing.

"See you around," Natalie said as her smile met her eyes.

I tried to respond but for some reason couldn't. So instead, I watched as she disappeared around the corner, leaving me alone with my thoughts and left in a daze.

Chapter Two
{Friday, October 13th, 2017}

"Good to have you back," my boss, Wayne, said to me before exiting the conference room.

I closed the folder in front of me as our client, Shelly, gathered her things as well.

"I was so glad to hear you were back," she said, stopping a few feet shy of me.

I garnered up a smile, but I wasn't sure how to respond.

"We were going to re-landscape last year," she continued. "But then you went on leave and, well, we decided to wait."

"I appreciate that, but we're a team here. You would've been in good hands."

"Team or not, I know you're the genius behind the particular projects we want to model ours after."

"Well, thank you," I said, extending my hand to her.

She took it. "Just don't go taking any more leaves until we wrap this project up. Got it?" she replied with a chuckle.

"Nothing to worry about there. The wife can only die from cancer once."

Her expression fell.

Fuck.

"I'm sorry," I realizing I had, in fact, just said that out loud to a client.

"No need," she began, but side-eyed the exit.

"Can I walk you out?" I asked.

"Oh, no, that's okay. I should be able to retrace my steps."

She gave a polite smile, trying to hide the look of horror in her eyes.

Wayne was going to kill me.

Shelly left the room, and as soon as she did, I fell back into my chair.

One week back and I had potentially fucked up my first project.

"You're the genius. She was waiting for you."

Was Natalie right? Was my supposed genius enough to keep her from pulling the plug on the whole thing?

I flipped the folder back open, eyeing pictures of the space they were looking to redesign.

I came to the third page where I had started sketching ideas while Shelly was talking. I had been a doodler in school, and that had continued into meetings. Sometimes I even did it in my daydream state. My head was often up in the clouds, but lately it had been spending a lot more time in my past rather than planning a future.

"God, you look—" I began, trying to recover my breath that had left me the moment I saw Natalie in her royal blue homecoming dress. It tied around her neck and hugged her chest tightly, flowing down to about mid-thigh.

"I think you're looking for the word 'gorgeous,'" Natalie said as she did a little twirl.

"I don't think there's a word to describe how beautiful you look."

"Damn, he's a smooth talker," Natalie's mom, Teresa, said as she joined us in the living room.

But I didn't know how to take her inflection.

"Cool it, Mom. He's just being sweet," she said, not taking her eyes away from mine.

"So, any plans after the dance?" Teresa asked.

My eyes widened a bit, I didn't know what she had told her mom.

"Yeah, we're going over to Shane's after, but I should be home by midnight."

"Okay," Teresa said, stepping towards Natalie and wrapping her daughter in an embrace. *"Remember, if you drink, call me for a ride."*

"I will, but I don't plan on it."

My eyes shifted between the two. I was certain my parents knew I had consumed alcoholic beverages a few times, but we didn't talk about it. I thought it was an unspoken rule between parents and kids?

"You got condoms, kid?"

"What?" I asked, my eyes widening enough that I was certain they were protruding from my head.

"Jesus, Mom, you're going to give him a heart attack," Natalie said trying to contain a smile.

I let my expression settle. "I have no need for them, ma'am," I replied, like I was responding to my mom.

"Ah—raw doggin' it," Teresa said.

"Oh, God—okay, we're leaving," Natalie said with an eye roll as she grabbed me by the arm.

"Have fun, baby, but not too much," Teresa said as we walked outside.

"We won't," Natalie said. "Love ya."

Once in the car, Natalie pulled on her seat belt and glanced over at me. She appeared nervous. It was the first time I had really seen that look on her face.

I had only known her a couple of weeks, but I felt like I had memorized every expression that came across it.

"Everything okay?" I asked.

"I was about to ask you that."

My brows furrowed. "I'm sorry. Do I not seem okay?" Was I really showing how nervous I was?

"No, you seem fine," she replied with a laugh. "My mom's just a bit eccentric since my dad, you know, took off. I was worried she freaked you out."

"She seems fine to me."

"Good. She's typically not that forward—"

"Seriously, she was fine," I replied, putting my hand on hers. "I think she's really funny."

"Leo—Wayne wants to see you," Rachelle said as she poked her head into the conference room.

She was already gone before I realized what was said. But once I did, I sighed, closed the folder and headed to his office.

***

"What was that about?" Philip asked as I finished up in Wayne's office and shut the door, walking to mine.

"My brain trying to fuck up my job," I joked, or tried to anyway.

"What'd you do?"

I stepped into my office, and he followed me in. "Just some stupid comment I made to Shelly."

His brow furrowed. He knew I wasn't the type to say inappropriate things to clients. But who knew what I was capable of now?

"Forget about it. I just need some sleep," I stated.

"Why don't you just take a little more time off? I mean, it's only been a few weeks."

"Shut up. You just want lead on this project," I replied with a grin.

"Well, if you fuck up again, I might get it anyway," he retorted, cocking his head.

But like all my conversations lately, the buddy-buddy shit would end swiftly, making room for the sympathetic tone and expression to settle in.

"But seriously," he began right on cue. "A little more time couldn't hurt."

My lips pressed together in a firm line as I spotted Natalie's and my wedding photo on the corner of my desk.

I cleared my throat as my eyes met his. "What for? Nothing's changed. I have a mortgage and a life to pay for."

The matter of fact in my tone threw us both. Maybe more so him than me as I was going for the nonchalant demeanor.

Phillip rubbed the back of his neck, before grinning nervously. I could tell he wanted to say something more, but he didn't. And as I heard my office door close behind him, my eyes fell back to Natalie in the picture.

Her eyes pierced into mine from the small rectangle frame. She had the same excitement in them that captivated me the night I asked her to be my girlfriend.

Natalie's hair, that had been perfectly pinned up at the beginning of the homecoming dance, was now flowing down her shoulders. I laughed thinking about the people around her being pelted with bobby pins.

She danced with the most carefree nature as the people around her were paired off with their friends.

We were only a few weeks into school, and since she had met me on day one, she hadn't made much of an effort to talk to anyone else.

She spotted me and ran over as I handed her the water I had grabbed for us.

"Oh, thank god, I thought I was going to die of dehydration," she said before tipping back the cup.

"Please don't die on my watch. I would have a lot of explaining to do."

She laughed as she set the cup down on a table by us.

"You're not nearly as sweaty as you should be," she said with a large grin crossing her face.

"I think you're doing it enough for the two of us."

The hair on my neck stood up as I realized what I had just said.

"What? You don't like girls who are a sweaty mess?" she asked, raising her brow.

I smiled, loving her confidence. Or maybe she was just hiding her vulnerability.

"I've always said, the sweatier the better."

Her head fell back as she let out a laugh and then grabbed my hand. "Alrighty then, you asked for it!"

I tried to seem like I had some sense of rhythm as she continued to sway, not caring that she had none.

"What?" she asked, her eyes meeting mine.

"You're amazing," I exclaimed over the music.

"I know," she replied, rolling her eyes before letting a brief lull linger in the air.

"Will you be my girlfriend?" I shouted.

But the noise level wasn't needed because the DJ had taken that moment to switch to a slow song at a softer tone.

All the people in the vicinity looked at us, or that's what it seemed like anyway.

But as embarrassed as I felt, Natalie looked more confident than ever.

"Absolutely."

I grabbed the picture frame and opened my top drawer, tossing it inside and pushing it shut.

I had done the same to the one in our living room. I couldn't take seeing her every night as I lay awake. And since sleeping was only coming at the expense of my body shutting down, I was seeing it more often than I had been seeing the inside of my eyelids.

***

The microwave beeped just before I opened it and pulled out the last of my mom's frozen leftovers.

My fork pierced the lasagna as steam rolled off the top. I stared at the bite, hoping my saliva glands would do their job and make me feel excited for my favorite meal. But they didn't.

I shoveled the food into my mouth, both the scalding and still partially frozen parts until it was gone. I placed my plate in the sink and walked towards the bathroom.

"Great, back to leaving dirty plates? What? Does your mother live here now?"

I paused in the door frame, exhaling as I turned around and walked back to the sink.

I picked up my plate, rinsed it off, and then placed it in the dishwasher.

As soon as it was closed, I threw my hands up in front of me to show Natalie it was done, and then finished my walk to the bathroom.

I turned the shower nozzle all the way over to the hottest level. That had nothing to do with Natalie's scolding, or my current somber demeanor. That was just the way I liked my showers. Well, I liked them better with her, even though she wasn't a fan of the steaming water. But she wasn't in there, so scalding hot would have to do.

I unbuttoned my shirt, tossed it to the ground, and then pulled my undershirt over my head and did the same.

Pulling off my ring, I set it in Natalie's ring holder next to hers.

Her wedding band and engagement ring glistened in the light. I picked them up and ran my fingers over them. They looked worn. That's because they were.

I placed them back next to mine as I finished undressing and got into the shower.

Music blared from the speakers in the basement. Shouting erupted, almost louder than the song.

My hands shook as Natalie and I stood in the kitchen of our friend's house that was just off campus.

She was dressed as Lara Croft, and I had opted for a simple getup as a lumberjack. Everything was already a part of my wardrobe except the suspenders I had to buy.

"You ready to head back to the dorms, babe?" she asked, with a small grin appearing on her face.

She probably thought the alcohol was getting to me, but it wasn't. However, my nerves were in full effect.

I took a deep breath and reached into my pocket.

"Woooo!" a shirtless guy in a mask yelled as he ran through the kitchen to the basement door and then disappeared.

Natalie laughed while her head shook. "If that's not a sign that two a.m. is our cut-off, then I don't know what is."

I tried to smile, but the muscles in my lips were working against me.

"Are you okay?" she asked, her brows furrowing as she touched my arm.

My hand shook in my pocket against the small velvet bag.

"Natalie—"

"Yeah?" she asked.

I pulled the bag out of my pocket and handed it to her.

She took it from me, giving me a questionable expression as she opened it and let its contents fall into her hand.

"Leo—" Her eyes shot up to mine.

She held the ring between her thumb and index finger. The opal shimmering in the small kitchen light.

"I had it made for you while we were in Mexico. It was when I snuck off for a little while with Mark."

"That was months ago," she said with a chuckle.

I followed hers up with a nervous laugh. "I was trying to find the perfect time to ask," I said as I rubbed the back of my neck.

She glanced around the kitchen as music, laughter and drunken singing continued to rise from the basement.

Clearly, I hadn't picked the perfect time. My expression fell.

God, I was fucking the whole thing up. Maybe we weren't ready. Maybe 19 was too young.

"So, will ya?" I asked, not in the confident way I had rehearsed it for months.

"Of course," she replied, her eyes lighting up with excitement.

She threw her arms around me, kissing me like she had never kissed me before.

My phone rang from the bathroom counter as I toweled off. It was Diane. I made a mental note to call her back. Though, at the same time, I was very aware that mental notes for me were a thing of the past.

I tied the towel around my waist and slipped my ring back on. I avoided the mirror but knew I would need to look soon to trim up my beard. Or maybe I would just go somewhere to have it done. Then I could ask them to face me away from it. That wouldn't be weird, right?

I walked down the hall to my home office where I had moved my clothes a few weeks before Natalie had passed. At the time I said it was so I didn't bug her while getting dressed, but I could see it was fore-thought so that I didn't have to enter my bedroom once she was gone.

After pulling on my boxers, I slipped a t-shirt over my head.

I should have done a better job picking one out that didn't remind me of her. But the woman had worn every article of clothing I owned. Even my boxers sometimes. So it shouldn't have mattered.

However, with that particular shirt, it did.

"Babe, are you coming to bed anytime soon?" Natalie asked *from the doorway.*

I shook my head and kept my eyes on the computer screen.

I clicked on another link that was certain to lead me down the fifth rabbit hole I had been in for the past two hours.

Glancing at the time in the corner of the screen, I corrected my thought. It was the fifth rabbit hole since nine. I had been at it for five hours.

I smelled her perfume just before I felt her hands on my shoulders. They slowly made their way to the front of my body, rubbing against the fabric on top of my chest.

"Nothing's going to be solved in the middle of the night," she said to me, her tone soft and sympathetic. Almost like I had been the one handed the death sentence.

"Not if I sleep it won't," I retorted, paying no mind to her tone, or the fact I hadn't tried to soften mine.

Her hands moved back to my shoulders as she began to rub them.

I swallowed the lump in my throat and continued to read down the page, searching for the missing piece that both her specialists and the two we had seen for second and third opinions had missed.

"How about we sleep for a few hours, and then you can get back at this tomorrow?" she asked, as if she was bargaining with a child.

I shook my head, feeling the tears well up in my eyes. But I had been hellbent on not letting her see me cry. I needed to be strong. She needed me to figure it out.

I had failed her so many times before. I'd be damned if I was going to fail her now.

Her hands left my body, and it felt like I was suddenly ice cold without her touch.

Would that be what it felt like when she was gone? Would the world feel cold? Would I be cold? How was it possible that there was a life for me after her death?

Her footsteps creaked in the hallway as I took a deep breath to control my thoughts and again the tears that threatened to fall.

I returned my focus to the screen and clicked on another link at the bottom of the webpage.

I wasn't certain what I was looking for. A cure? A treatment plan that didn't end in death? A list of why these crazy fucking doctors were wrong and all three had misdiagnosed my wife?

I was certain I would find one of the three. It was the internet. It was the twenty-first century. And if I had learned anything from all the hours of Grey's Anatomy *she had made me watch, there was someone out there that could make all of this heartache go away.*

"Babe, I think we should talk about this," Natalie said as she sat down on the love seat against the wall in front of my desk.

I glanced up at her as she held a mug in her hands, blowing on the top of it as the steam dissipated into the air. Her hair was in a messy bun and one of my shirts she was always wearing hung flawlessly over her.

She tucked her perpetually cold feet underneath herself, letting her eyes meet mine as her sympathetic smile returned.

"What's there to talk about?" I asked, pulling my glance from hers and looking back at the screen.

"Leo," she began.

At some point she was going to lose her patience with me.

"Leo," she said again.

I looked up.

"We need to talk about this."

Her tone had lost its patience, but her eyes still held a sadness she hadn't been able to shake since getting the news.

I wished I could say the sadness was for herself. Then I would at least have had something to use to comfort her. But the sadness wasn't for the life she was losing, but for me having to lose her.

A tear splashed onto my arm.

Shit.

Hold yourself together.

That had been on repeat for a few weeks now. But each day, I was losing my grip just a little more.

"Leo," she said again.

Fuck, soon I wouldn't have to worry about her dying first. She was going to kill me.

I exhaled. "What do you want me to say?" I asked, my tone much harsher than I had intended.

But I didn't follow it up with any kind of apology. The anger pushed back the tears, and I welcomed the help.

She tilted her head. "Don't be like that."

"Shouldn't you be resting?" I asked, trying to sound a little less bitter, but I wasn't sure that was making it through.

"I would be, if you would come to bed."

"I'll come to bed once I have a way to get rid of the glioblastoma—"

"—Glen," she interjected.

I looked above my screen at her.

"I named him Glen," she replied with a smile. "At least Lydia has a friend now. She was being quite a bitch in her lonely state."

She giggled to herself.

My expression didn't change.

She sighed. She hated when I wasn't being fun. I hated when I wasn't being fun. But someone needed to be serious.

"How can you be so cavalier about this?" I asked.

"What do you want me to do, Leo? The doctors told us there's nothing they can do."

I rolled my eyes and ran my hand through my hair. "And you're just going to accept that?"

"Am I going to accept it when three different doctors tell me there's absolutely no way they can save me?" she asked rhetorically and then answered for herself. "Yes, I'm inclined to believe their years of experience and medical degrees."

I exhaled and rolled the chair back, getting to my feet, although I was unsure of where to storm off to. It was two a.m. and I had work in the morning.

"Leo, I don't want to spend what time I have left fighting with you."

"Then don't fight with me," I exclaimed. The tears that had been repressed for weeks finally broke through. "Why don't you fight Glen like you fight Lydia? Fight him like you fight me when I'm being a fucking asshole," I continued, a sob lodging itself in my throat. "Just fucking fight to stay with me!"

Natalie quickly made her way to me and wrapped her arms around my body.

She didn't tell me not to cry or to be strong, but instead held me like I should've been holding her.

"I promise I'll fight," she whispered through my labored breaths. "I promise I'll do everything I can to stay with you."

My phone's ringtone replaced the sound of my wife's gentle voice.

I glanced over at my desk where the sound was coming from, noticing that from my angle I had ended up on the ground at some point in my trip down memory lane.

The phone stopped before I made my way to it. That time it was my mom.

I took another mental note. One that I already knew would be forgotten.

Chapter Three
{Thursday, November 16th, 2017}

"Did you get the new sketches up for the Pennival account?" Wayne asked from the doorway of my office.

"Yeah, I turned them over to Cindy an hour ago."

"Perfect. So what are you still doing here?"

"Just getting started on some stuff for next week."

Wayne rolled his eyes. "Leo, remember what we talked about?"

"What does me working late have to do with that?"

"You have to blow off steam. You came back to work before you were ready—"

"I—"

"Nope," he interjected. "Not up for discussion. I understand this keeps you busy. And busy is good right now. But busy is just a distraction. And you will hit a wall. I'm just trying to prevent you from being injured when that happens."

"What could a wall possibly do to me at this point?" I replied bitterly.

"That's exactly what I'm talking about, Leo. You're not letting yourself grieve, and it will catch up to you."

"Wayne, I'm grieving—I've *grieved*. Maybe it's just different to everyone because I had a whole year to process her death before it happened. But I'm fine. Really. I just want to get ahead of everything before next week."

"Well, do it from your house then. I'm not aiding in your denial past the five o'clock mark."

My eyes narrowed, but what was I supposed to say? He was my boss and could have easily fired my ass a few times already.

"Fine, I'll work from my home office."

"Well, I can't stop you there. But I really think you should try and do something fun for your birthday instead of spending it working," Wayne said before walking away.

"Happy birthday dear Leo, Happy birthday to you!" my family sang as my mom set the cake with seventeen candles on it down in front of me.

"Make a wish," Natalie said as she squeezed my knee under the table.

I glanced over at her.

What was there left to wish for?

I smiled at her.

"Make a wish already! You're getting wax on the cake!" my little brother, Grant, exclaimed.

Natalie laughed as I turned from her and blew them out.

Everyone clapped like the act of blowing out candles was a victorious moment.

My mom grabbed the cake and cut the pieces as my dad grabbed the plates.

Natalie squeezed my knee again, bringing my attention back to her.

"I have a surprise for you," she whispered, eyeing my mom carefully and then glancing back at me.

Her whisper, along with the mischievous look in her eyes, made me excited. Her hand on my knee didn't hurt either.

"Can we get away?" she asked, keeping her tone the same.

"Ah, Mom? Can we take off for a little bit?"

"And not eat cake?" she asked, her brows furrowing.

I glanced at Natalie, unsure if the surprise came with time restrictions.

"Oh, there's always time for cake," Natalie assured.

My mom smiled and handed us both a piece.

I did my best to not inhale the dessert, but it was possible I did, and my mom noticed. However, I was certain it was because she assumed she had outdone herself this year when baking it.

"Great cake, Mom. Are we good?"

My mom glanced over at my dad who looked to be holding in a laugh.

"Yes, yes. Go be seventeen," she said, waving her hand in the air.

Again, I tried not to rush. I tried to walk slow. But even if there wasn't a surprise involved, I was always excited for anytime I got alone with Natalie.

I grabbed my keys as we slipped on our shoes.

"Do you mind if I drive?" she asked.

Without hesitation I held the keys out to her, and she took them.

"So, do I get to know where we're going?" I asked as we reached my car.

She shook her head. *"Nope, it's a surprise."*

"Does it have anything to do with the bag you brought?" I asked, eyeing the duffle she had left in my car when I had picked her up before dinner.

"Yes," she replied as we got in and shut the door. *"But no more questions. You'll see what I have planned soon enough."*

I sighed, gathering the papers I would need to review at home where I couldn't be attacked for being a dedicated employee. The papers, while not thoroughly exciting, could help me try to forget that none of my birthdays would ever be as good as they once had been.

***

I pulled my car into the garage and turned it off. Glancing around, I took in the bland sight of the dull gray color of the walls and now empty shelving as I had packed everything away after my outburst the day she had died.

"You should go out and do something."

Her voice released the tension in my shoulders for a moment before it promptly returned with her silence.

I looked towards the door to the house. Every night when I came home, I expected to walk in and see her. Like everything had just been a cruel joke and she was just on vacation. I hated that hope. I hated that every night I had to relive the same sadness. I hated even more that every day I had the same thought.

I got out of the car and walked to my door, unlocking it. Again, the thought of her on the other side of it flashed through my mind.

Her waiting patiently for me in her birthday suit, or a new teddy she had bought, or a giant cake that we couldn't possibly finish just the two of us.

My body froze as I heard movement on the other side of the door.

It was brief; it was quiet; it was probably a mouse or a robber. But maybe—just maybe—it was her and my hoping and wishing had been right.

I quickly turned the knob and stepped in, hoping with everything in me to either be shot by a thief or feel the warmth of my wife's body against mine.

Unfortunately, I got neither.

"Surprise!" I heard from a variety of voices before I saw any faces.

The light clicked on and a group of about twenty people stood in my house.

Twenty people that I knew. Twenty people that I liked. Twenty people that I wished would get the fuck out.

"Sorry, it was Beth's idea," Mark said as he walked up to me.

I gave a forced smile. I don't think I was hiding the forced part well.

"What are you guys doing in town?" I asked, clearly leaving my manners in the car.

"We're actually moving back. Well, I am first. Then Beth will follow once everything is settled back home. But my new job starts in two weeks."

"Oh, wow."

I meant to continue into a congratulations, but Beth approached at that moment.

"How ya holdin' up?" she asked, with no soft lead-in.

"Ah, fine," I glanced around. All twenty people stared at me. Or it felt like they were anyway. If they weren't, it's because they were forcing themselves not to. "I need a minute," I stated.

"Take two," Mark joked.

I thought Beth was going to deck him for that one. I certainly wanted to. But I was already heading down the hall before what he said was fully registered.

I shut the bathroom door and leaned my back up against it. I took a deep breath, as the adrenaline was either settling down from the possibility of finally seeing Natalie or ramping up because, instead of her, I got a room full of people who weren't my wife.

"You brought me to school?" I asked as my brows furrowed.

She laughed at my expression. "Yeah, we don't spend nearly enough time here," she replied, opening her door as I followed suit.

After she grabbed the duffle bag, I followed her, walking a short way to the football field.

"Is my birthday the *event?" I asked with a grin, thinking back to the first time we talked.*

"It is," she replied, taking my hand in hers.

Excitement hit me again.

The parking lot lights that had illuminated our walk dissipated as we entered the football field.

Natalie unzipped the bag and pulled out two large blankets that left me wondering how in the hell she had fit them in there. Or more so, how she was going to get them back in.

She laid one out on the ground and then rested the other on top of it.

Our own little bed. That thought excited me just as much.

She reached into the bag again.

"Jesus, Mary Poppins, there's more in there?"

She laughed as she pulled out two books and small battery-operated lantern.

"Now for the main event," she said as she handed me Pride and Prejudice *and kept the other for herself. "I'm sorry I couldn't buy you anything. Money's a little tight right now with my parents' divorce."*

Her excitement in the moment wavered a little at her words.

I stepped over to her and tipped her chin up to look at me. "This is perfect," I replied.

And I meant it. It was *perfect.*

She pushed up from her heels and let her lips briefly touch mine. Then she took my hand and led me to the blanket.

We used the second one as a pillow, keeping in mind that, at some point, the temperature would shift, and we would need it to stay warm. But after a little while of reading, I was too busy focusing on her body right next to mine to care about ever being cold again.

"You're supposed to be reading," she said with a giggle.

"Sorry, I'm having a hard time concentrating," I confessed.

She set the book, Tuesdays with Morrie, *down and turned her body towards mine.*

That wasn't going to help my distraction.

"Which part did you make it to?" she asked.

I rested the book on my chest and looked at her.

"It is a truth universally acknowledged, that a single man in possession of a good fortune must be in want of a wife," I quoted.

She smiled. She loved when I quoted books.

"What has you distracted?" she asked, her look turning mischievous which always just excited me more.

"The same thing that's had me distracted for the past few months."

"And that is?" she asked, knowing the answer but wanting to hear it anyway.

"You," I replied as I shifted and kissed her forehead.

Her eyes remained shut for a moment as she seemed to hold on to the feeling of my lips.

"Would you read to me?" she asked.

My brow lifted. "You want me to read Pride and Prejudice *to you?"*

She nodded, snuggling up against my body, her eyes shutting. "I love your voice. It's soothing."

How could I say no to that? I smiled as I picked up the book. "It is a truth universally acknowledged, that a single man in possession of a good fortune must be in want of a wife—" I began.

I read to her for hours underneath the stars. The air had grown colder, but our bodies pressed together were all the warmth we needed.

"We should probably get going," I said as I rested the book on my chest and tucked a lock of hair behind her ear.

"Two more minutes," she whispered without opening her eyes.

I smiled. "Okay, two more minutes."

"Leo?" I heard in tandem with a knock on the bathroom door.

I glanced in the mirror, wiping my glossed-over eyes.

"Uh, yeah. One sec," I said, trying to prevent myself from sniffling too loud.

I opened the door. Tabatha. She did a better job concealing her sympathy than Beth had done. Or really anyone. But that didn't surprise me. Tabatha seemed to get people more than they got her.

"Not checking on you; just needed to pee," she said with a smirk.

"Well, there *are* two other bathrooms in this place," I replied, hoping the tone conveyed my attempt at a witty response.

"This one's my favorite."

"Mine too. Something about the beautiful stonework that just draws you in."

"See, you get it," she exclaimed with a laugh.

No, *she* got it. She knew I didn't want to be checked on. I didn't want to be asked for the billionth time if I was okay or if I needed anything. Because she knew that, even if I did, I sure as hell wasn't going to ask.

"Well, it's all yours. I'm going to go change," I said, turning towards the office instead of the living room.

She nodded, doing the polite thing Tabatha did which was not to question *why* I was heading in the opposite direction of my bedroom.

"Holy shit. Someone got him away from the office long enough to celebrate his birthday!" Mark exclaimed as I approached everyone at the table in the restaurant

"Shut up," I replied, hitting his back and then going in for a hug.

He laughed and Beth followed suit with a hug of her own.

"Is Natalie coming?" Ethan asked from across the table.

I shrugged. "She's been working a lot lately too. Guess we'll see," I said with no real inflection.

No one responded to that. Why would they? My wife and I were busy. We both had jobs. We both had full workloads. That didn't need to be explained.

"What're you drinking?" Mark asked as I took the open seat beside him and across from Tabatha, Ethan's newest girlfriend.

"I probably shouldn't. I have work in the morning."

"We all have work in the morning," Mark replied. "Come on. One drink."

I rolled my eyes as the waitress walked up.

"Gin and tonic please," I said to her.

"Attaboy," Mark said as he ordered a round of shots for the table.

"So, how old are you now?" Tabatha asked.

"Twenty-eight."

"I just turned thirty-one earlier this year. I thought I would miss my twenties, but nope. Thirties is where it's at."

"What changes?" Beth asked like we were getting a peek into another realm.

"Priorities," she replied with a shrug. "I guess your outlook and not needing to be with someone."

I looked up at her, but Mark spoke.

"Big words for someone who has a boyfriend."

She laughed, but it felt kind of forced. "I like being with Ethan. But I don't need to be with Ethan. There's a difference."

Mark raised a brow. He didn't get it. But neither did I.

"Ethan and I have our own lives. We make our own money and do our own things. We like hanging out. So that's the difference. We want each other. We don't need each other."

Beth looked to Mark. "Do you need me or want me?"

"Trick question," Mark replied as the waitress dropped off my drink and the shots.

"No, it's not," Beth retorted.

I withheld an eye roll. I was certain they were going to get into it again. I wanted to tell Mark to just shut up and tell his wife that he wanted her. Because, with the wisdom Tabatha was trying to share with us, I was certain that was what Beth was wanting to hear.

But I was no longer an expert in that department. My wife had been slowly slipping away from me for the better part of two years, and I was just letting her. I wasn't showing that I wanted or needed her.

"There she is!" Mark exclaimed.

I looked up to see Natalie dressed in a navy-blue dress with matching heels. It was a little dressier than what she usually wore to work, so I briefly wondered if she had stopped home to change. Was she dressing up for me?

What would she say if I asked her if I was a need or want? Or was I neither at that point? Had we passed the needs and wants, and run right into obligation?

"Okay, so this was a bad idea," Mark said as he found me sitting in my office chair.

"What?" I asked, but then realized what he had said. "No, ah, it's fine. I just needed a minute."

He looked at his watch. "Well, it's been an hour, and everyone felt weird, so they all took off."

"Shit," I said with a sigh as I shook my head. "I'm sorry. I've been kind of spacey lately."

He exhaled and then sat on the corner of my desk. "It's completely understandable, man. No one blames you."

"I know, but I *would* like to see everyone. I just don't think I'm ready."

He put his hand on my shoulder. "And we'll be here when you are."

Would they? They had left before. They had left when we were best friends. Why come back? Why be there for me now?

"Mark," I said as he stood up.

"Hmm?"

"What happened years ago between us? Why'd you leave?"

His reaction wasn't what I had expected—a smile.

"Ah, you know," he began as he chuckled. "Friends grow apart; people get busy. The usual."

"Busy? Overnight?"

He chuckled once more. "Overnight? Man, you must be getting old. Memory going already?" He shook his head, clearly unphased by how I thought things had gone.

Was I remembering it wrong? Had we been drifting like Natalie and I had been drifting before that? Or did my push into working on things with Natalie push Mark out because I no longer had the time to juggle my best friend, my wife, *and* my career?

Had I been the bad guy the whole time? Should I have reached out?

"Hey, Mark," I began as he walked to the door.

"Yeah, bud?"

"Thanks for coming."

He looked back at me and smiled. "I'm always here for ya."

And for the first time in years, I wondered if he always had been, and I just hadn't been there for him.

***

After Mark and Beth left, I picked up the few things they had left behind and remade my bed on the couch.

One of them had undoubtedly seen it. Someone had to have moved it. I was certain that fueled some of the sympathetic looks. Poor Leo. He can't even sleep in his own bed.

But what about the guest rooms? I imagined one asking the other.

Well, they've fucked in all those, too, they would retort.

Oh, but not the couch?

Not this one. It was a new couch. They didn't get to break it in.

Sad.

Very sad.

Poor Leo.

Oh, look, Mark and Beth brought appetizers into a house they broke into to surprise a man who hates surprise parties.

I shook my head at the absurdity of the conversation I had concocted in my head.

"You should have changed the code years ago. Besides, I don't think their conversation went quite like that."

I smirked. "Well, since you're a ghost now, you can spill the goods. What'd they say?"

Her voice didn't answer. The corners of my lips fell. Why was she teasing me? Talking to me and then leaving me? Making jokes and then disappearing before we got to the punchline.

I bunched up my pillow, preparing to make another sleepless night a little more comfortable for my head. Though comfort was barely a thing anymore, and I was certain it wouldn't be again.

Natalie's body nestled tighter to mine—if that was even possible. The only way I could sleep was with her clutched in my arms. She didn't seem to care that I was a space heater like she had for all the years before. She embraced the warmth. Because with warmth, there was life.

She nestled in again. She was testing the waters to see if I was in the mood.

Who was I to deny my wife's wish to fuck me on my *birthday? On the last one she would be alive for.*

I moved my hand from the bed in front of her and put it on her hip, slowly running it down her thigh and then back up.

She took a deep, longing breath.

I shifted my face into the back of her neck and kissed it. My beard rubbing against her skin made her giggle.

My fingers lifted the fabric to her underwear as I teased along the edges.

She pushed her ass into me, doing some teasing of her own.

I kissed her shoulders, letting my lips linger a little longer each time.

Her body shifted as she turned to face me, my hand feeling the fabric of the sheet once again instead of her.

She playfully pushed me onto my back and climbed on top, straddling me.

I reached up and placed my hands on the outside of her white tank top that I could see her nipples through.

She moved away just a little as she put her hands on the lining of my boxers and maneuvered them down my thighs.

She grabbed her hair and pulled it out of her way as she took me in her mouth.

I moaned, my hand replacing hers on her head as I gripped her hair.

"Fuck," I said in between moans, trying to keep my eyes open so I could watch her.

God was she beautiful—and not just because of what she was doing.

The thought of this being the last birthday I might spend with her sprang tears to my eyes. And I panicked.

This was not the time or the place.

I tugged at her arm and did some maneuvering of my own to be on top of her.

I couldn't risk taking a quick pause for her to remove her underwear, scared that I would let another horrible thought cross my mind. So I shifted the fabric over and pushed inside of her, letting us moan in tandem with one another.

She gripped my shoulders, kissing every inch of my skin she could reach.

But I just wanted my lips on hers. I wanted to see her, to feel her, to have her. Forever.

Chapter Four
{Sunday, December 24th, 2017}

I had successfully skipped Thanksgiving with my family. Lying shamelessly about spending it with Natalie's mom, Teresa, instead.

Although I didn't have to worry about Teresa being lonely for the holidays since she had met and seemingly fallen madly in love with someone in the few months since Natalie had passed.

I was certain it wasn't love in the way she was wanting it, but rather needing it. However, that was for her therapist to sort out, not her son-in-law. Former son-in-law? Regardless, not for me.

I was hoping the normal two-hour flight to my parents for Christmas would take longer than that, but there were no delays, no wait times, no slowing down a speeding train into my past.

"Leo!" my mom exclaimed as she opened the door and wrapped her arms around me.

"Merry Christmas Eve," I said half-heartedly, but trying as much as I could for my mom.

"Merry Christmas Eve, honey," she said back as she held the side of my arms, a foot apart from me, and sized me up.

I looked different. Just say it. We both knew it.

She smiled with her lips—not her eyes—but said nothing.

"Are your things in the car?" she asked.

I nodded, taking off my coat.

"You're staying, right?"

I nodded once more. "Yeah, I'll grab them a little later."

I took off my boots and followed her the rest of the way in.

My aunt and uncle sat on the couch in the living room looking deep in conversation with my dad.

"Look who's here!" my Mom said with excitement ringing from her voice.

"Hey, Leo!" my uncle exclaimed but didn't stand up.

My aunt however jumped to her feet and pulled me in for a warm embrace. "How have you been, dear?"

It wasn't an unusual question for people to ask in general, but I no longer knew how to answer when asked. Because even if I said—and meant—that I was fine, no one believed me.

"I'm good. Work's been busy. Lots of new projects to design."

"Sounds wonderful! We'll have to get down there and see them."

"That would be great," I replied the same way I always had.

But my aunt and uncle didn't travel. They barely left the county, let alone the state. It was why I understood their absences from Natalie's funeral.

"Where's Grant?" I asked.

My mom glanced towards the stairs. "He's up in his room."

I nodded at my dad, who clearly didn't want to treat me any differently than the other holidays I had come home for, which I appreciated.

I walked up the stairs and pushed Grant's door open from the inch it had been cracked.

"Hey, I heard you moved back," I said leaning up against the door frame.

"Yeah, well, not all businesses work out."

I nodded, glancing around. I hadn't meant it as a tease, but I was sure he had taken it that way.

"I'm only here for a few months," he continued. "Just until I can save up enough money to get my own place."

"No harm in that."

I glanced over at my side of the room, or what had been my side growing up anyway.

"You could always sell that big place of yours and move back in here with me and the 'rents," he added.

I rolled my eyes. "I'll pass."

"How about we just swap? Mom said you aren't using most of the house anyway."

I shrugged. "I've just been working a lot."

"Yeah, that's what she said too."

I wanted to invite him to come stay with me, have someone to use the space I couldn't. But he had barely talked to me since Natalie had gotten sick. Since we had told the family the year before.

He had flown in the day she died. But while I was in the garage falling apart, he had taken off, and I hadn't heard from him since. Not even for the funeral.

"Are you high?" he asked.

I lifted my brow.

He shrugged at my expression. "You seem out of it—thought maybe you started medicating."

I shook my head.

"Well, I can get you something if you need it. The holidays might be brutal otherwise."

"Noted," I replied before eyeing a Batman poster on the wall that I had left behind when leaving for college. I hadn't realized Grant never took it down.

"You left that up?" I asked, tipping my head towards it.

He smiled, but it wavered. "Yeah, I thought it was kind of a staple to our room. I couldn't change everything after you left."

I nodded, staring at the poster as a pain settled into my chest.

I took a deep breath and walked into the hallway as the feeling intensified. I leaned up against the wall, trying to catch the breath I hadn't even noticed I had lost.

"The wood creaks right in front of my parents' door, so take a big step over it," I said to Natalie over the phone. *"Then shift to the left right under the picture frame and then an immediate move to the right. You should be good after that."*

"Why does sneaking into your house seem like a goddamn diamond heist?"

I laughed.

"Shhhh," she replied. *"You don't want to wake them before I even get in there."*

"Sorry."

"Okay, well, I'll be there in a few," she added. *"But my minutes are almost out on my phone. So, I'll see you soon."*

I hung up and stared out the window in anticipation of her arrival.

Grant was staying the weekend with a friend, and Natalie's mom was visiting her brother a few towns over. Natalie said she had a school project to work on. I was certain Teresa knew she was lying.

I had told Natalie I would lie and say I was staying somewhere else and go to her place. Her response was that my mom would call and check up on me. And she was right; she would. So, sneaking her into my bed seemed like the safer option.

After a few minutes, I saw her appear from behind the trees in the front drive. I was having a really hard time controlling my excitement. I hoped that the one I had rubbed out in the shower earlier that day would be enough for me to keep my cool.

I stood by my door, quietly opening it so I could watch for her in the hallway.

When she came up the stairs, she took a big step in front of my parents' door, shifted left by the picture frame and then immediately went to the right. No creaks. No problems.

Her eyes met mine.

I opened the door all the way for her like she was entering a grand hotel instead of the bedroom I shared with my brother.

I closed the door, holding steady, worried that even a click would wake the overlords and my princess would be hauled away from me.

But Natalie didn't have the same level of control. Her body was on mine the second I stepped away from the door. Her tongue slipped into my mouth as my hand got lost in her hair.

After a minute, she pulled away. "I missed you," she stated.

"It's been like three hours since I've seen you," I replied breathlessly.

But we both knew that didn't matter. It could have been minutes and it still would have felt like an eternity.

She slipped off her shoes and socks and tucked them under the bed. Then she took off her jeans and folded them, placing them in the same spot.

I cleared my throat. I hadn't seen her in her underwear before. We hadn't made it past the under-the-shirt feel-up. Which I was fine with. But her standing there in just a shirt and underwear told me I should have taken a few extra showers that afternoon.

"Sorry, I sleep better pants-less."

I nodded, trying to think of something clever to say. But I was broken from my concentration of what to say by her climbing into my bed.

"Are you going to be joining me?"

I also slept pants-less, but I wasn't sure if that little of fabric between us was a great idea. Not that the thin material of my pajama pants was going to stop the thoughts, but I was hoping it would restrain my excitement for her from showing too much.

I lifted the covers, sneaking a peek at her thighs and purple laced underwear one more time before I joined her underneath.

"Your bedsheets smell like lavender," she said with a grin.

"Yeah, I washed them this afternoon."

"For me? What a gentleman."

I laughed. "You don't have very high standards."

"I'd disagree. I think I have some of the highest."

"You're with me, in a room that has a Batman Returns *poster on the wall."*

She glanced up at it. "Any man who idolizes Michael Keaton is top notch in my book."

"Ah, so he's what does it for ya?" I joked.

She grinned, her eyes lingering into mine. "Nope, only you."

"Hey, you good?" Grant asked, startling me.

The ache in my chest had stopped in my time away but had started south of that.

I took a deep breath. "Ah, yeah. Just need a minute," I said before I stepped into the bathroom and shut the door.

Why did any gathering of people result in hiding in a bathroom? Probably because no one could follow me there. Maybe I should just camp out in the tub for the remainder of Christmas. Maybe even the remainder of my life.

I exhaled before splashing some water on my face. I hadn't thought about what a whole other trip down memory lane my parents' house would be. I had been stuck in the past for months, reliving every bit of our life we had gone through, moment by moment.

When would it stop?

I knew the answer to that. It would stop once the memory-making did. Once her life ended. When the old memories would be lost, and the newest ones would be too faded to be clear.

Would there ever be a time?

Or maybe I would be perpetually stuck in the past. Maybe I had died and gone to hell. Maybe I was living in some kind of purgatory. I had seen *What Dreams May Come*. But was I Robin Williams or Annabella Sciorra? Certainly I had to be Annabella. Dark thoughts. Dark space. Bright memories that held a dark cloud over them now.

"Leo—" My Mom said through the door with a light knock.

I opened it before she tried again.

"Dinner's ready," she continued, her eyes trying hard to hide their sympathy.

"Perfect. I'm starving," I replied in the most chipper tone I had used in months. Clearly, I was overcompensating for how dark my thoughts had just gotten. But she didn't see that. She only saw her son excited for her cooking like he always used to be. And that thrilled her to no end.

***

"So, have you thought about moving back here?" my aunt asked.

After a moment of silence, I looked up, my mouth full of stuffing. I swallowed it and then replied. "Me?"

She smiled politely as my uncle chuckled. "Yes, you, dear. They're doing a lot of improvement to the scenery in town. Not just here, but throughout the whole state."

"How would she know? They never leave."

I sighed at Natalie's response. Now wasn't the time to be hearing from her. I couldn't risk a breakdown in front of my mother.

But my sigh was ill-timed. My aunt thought it was aimed at her.

"I'm sorry, Leo, I just meant—"

"Oh, no, that wasn't to you."

But that didn't help. Either it was to her, or it was to my dead wife. And that was crazy, right?

"I mean, I just don't know what I'm doing," I began again, trying to fix it.

"Isn't that the truth," Grant said, slightly under his breath.

I glanced over at him.

"Grant," my mom scolded.

"Says the guy fresh off a failed business," my dad retorted in my defense.

"Roger!"

Grant's posture in his chair reflected more of a teenager than the twenty-seven-year-old man he was. His black hoodie at Christmas dinner certainly didn't help.

"What?" he said bitterly to me.

I hadn't realized I was staring.

"Grant, stop being a jackass," my dad said.

"Roger, don't call him that," my mom retorted.

"Why? He's actin' like one."

I chose not to say anything and instead looked down at my plate. My mom had outdone herself. I knew she hated the time spent in the kitchen, especially since there was more food than the mouths could eat every year. But this year was different. She wanted to make sure she didn't miss a beat in giving me a full stomach each day I was home.

"Jesus, are you even still in there?" I heard Grant ask.

Again, it took a minute to realize someone was talking to me. But I didn't need to ask that time. His eyes searing into mine told me exactly who his words were aimed at.

"Grant, leave your brother alone," my mom said like when we were kids.

"No, he needs to snap out of it!" he exclaimed, leaning against the edge of the table. "It's been months, Leo. She's gone! She's not coming back!"

My dad's hand hit the table as our silverware clanked against our plates.

"Grant!" my mom exclaimed when I said nothing. "What is wrong with you? Why would you say that?"

Grant shifted back in his seat and stood up. "Somebody needed to tell him. And you all sure as hell weren't going to do it."

I watched as he left the room, but I again said nothing.

"Leo?" my mom asked, causing my eyes to drift her way. "Are you okay?"

I nodded and poked a piece of ham with my fork before inserting it into my mouth in place of an audible response.

"They're here!" Natalie exclaimed as I pulled the ham out of the oven and set it on the stove.

"Great. I'm starving."

"We can't just start eating. I put some crackers out for everyone first."

"I'm pretty sure they'll want more than crackers."

She shot me a look. "I put some dip out for them, too."

I grinned at her excitement—and well, nervousness—at hosting our first Christmas in our apartment.

My parents were visiting Grant in New York at school, so we invited a misfit of people. Teresa, Mark, Beth, Diane, and Diane's boyfriend.

"Hey!" Beth exclaimed as soon as she was in the door.

"Hi!" Natalie replied, beaming in all of her hostess glory.

"It smells amazing in here," Beth commented.

"It better. We've been cooking all day," I retorted.

"Shit, you let that man cook?" Mark asked, next in line to hug Natalie.

"We're doing it together," Natalie reiterated.

"I've mostly just watched," I said. "There's just something about a woman in the kitchen."

"Sexist pig," Diane said as she walked in the front door. She winked at me as Mark made his way over to me in the kitchen.

"Who's the poor S.O.B with Diane?" Mark whispered to me.

"Her boyfriend—Jared? Jason? Jesse?"

"This is Joseph," we overheard Diane say to Natalie and Beth.

I snapped my finger. "So close."

Mark laughed.

"And be nice. Diane's great," I continued.

"Diane's scary."

"Only because she doesn't submit to you and your dashing good looks."

"Dashing, you say?" he asked, raising a brow.

"I wonder why the dislike is mutual between the two of you," I said sarcastically.

"Nah, that has nothing to do with it. Natalie doesn't fawn over me, and I like her."

"Natalie isn't single. Nor will she ever be," I retorted.

"Confidence from my man, Leo. I like it. It suits you," he said with his hand falling onto my shoulder.

"Oh, God, what toxic masculinity bullshit is going on in here?" Diane asked as she put a six pack of beer into the fridge.

I shook my head and concealed a laugh. Mark wasn't as amused by her words.

"Well, Merry Christmas to you, too," he said, reaching past her and grabbing one of my beers from the fridge.

"Oh, sure, help yourself," I said to him.

"Hey, it's the season of giving. Besides, you're up for that big promotion. It's only a matter of time before you're making the big bucks and can afford more than this shitty beer."

***

After dinner, I volunteered to do the dishes so my parents could talk with my aunt and uncle. More so that I didn't have to. But that was an easy tell at that point.

My uncle popped his head into the kitchen and waved goodbye before heading out to start up the car. My aunt, however, had me stop doing the dishes so she could hold me in her embrace. She said she had read that there were medicinal properties in hugs lasting longer than twenty seconds. My counting must have been faster than hers. But the sentiment was sweet.

When I finished the dishes, I headed up the stairs stopping just outside of my brother's room—our room? I grimaced at the closed door. I wasn't sure what I was going to say to him. I wasn't sure what he was looking for.

"He's not in there," my mom said as she stepped out of the bathroom.

I glanced at her.

"He took off about an hour ago."

"Oh, did he say where he was going?"

"No, probably just blowing off steam. He's got a lot on his mind."

I nodded.

I'd like to say the feeling was mutual, but I hadn't really had a lot on my mind. My mind itself was foggy. So if there was a lot going on in there, I didn't know it.

"Do you want help getting your stuff?" she asked.

I shook my head. "Thanks though."

***

I grabbed my suitcase out of the car and walked back into the house and to the guest bedroom. Although we had multiple rooms in the house, mom had stuck the two of us in the same room growing up. She was worried we wouldn't bond because of the five-year age gap. I think the close quarters made things worse.

I tossed the bag onto the guest bed, suddenly feeling drained of all energy.

It had been months since I had slept more than two straight hours. I knew it would catch up to me. But why now?

I took a seat on the bed next to the bag, putting my head in my hands. I ran them across my face back and forth a few times until I let them move through my hair.

Turning to unzip my bag, I took out the little gift-wrapped box and held it to my chest as I fell back the rest of the way on the bed. My head fell half on the pillow and my feet stayed planted on the floor in front of me.

I was tired enough that I was certain I could sleep in that position. But the lack of comfort would have nothing to do with me waking up just shortly after. I could be sleeping on a damn cloud and I still wouldn't have a restful night's sleep.

The next day was Christmas.

The day for miracles to happen.

At least that was what all my favorite childhood movies taught me.

I would wake up in the morning to my wife downstairs. To her smiling face, beaming at the Pride and Prejudice Necklace I had bought for her the month before in one of my bouts of online shopping in the middle of another sleepless night.

It was also why I was the owner of three different pastel-colored toasters I knew she would like. Those were amongst other things that were waiting for her back home if a Christmas miracle did come true.

"I wanted to thank everyone for coming," Natalie said with a big smile on her face.

She had been practicing that face for months. Only on me. Since I was the only one who knew. But she had gotten good at hiding her sadness. I knew she thought she needed to—for me. And well, she wasn't exactly wrong.

My family sat on one side of our dining room table—Mom, Dad, Grant and his girlfriend. And on the other was Natalie's mom, Teresa, Teresa's brother and his wife, and Diane. They could all tell something was up. But as I had suspected would happen, they were expecting good news, not the news we were preparing to share.

But this was how Natalie wanted to do it. One giant band-aid.

And it was her news to share. Who was I to say that they should be told one by one? That it shouldn't happen on a holiday as it could ruin it for someone?

I was certain she had thought of all of that too, but she was worried she would chicken out and not tell them. Then she would die. And they wouldn't have gotten to say their goodbyes.

Maybe that was better. Maybe I wished I didn't know either.

Natalie had continued on with her rehearsed speech, but I had clearly let my mind take me away. She reached over for my hand as hers shook. I gripped it tightly in mine. She was losing her nerve.

"Oh, just tell us already," Grant joked. "Did ya finally knock her up?" he asked, looking at me.

My parents beamed along with Teresa, hoping those were the words about to leave her mouth.

Natalie's hand went limp in mine. "I can't do this," she whispered to me, but she might as well have said it to the whole table, because they all heard anyway. "Will you?" she asked. But it wasn't really a request because she fled the room in no time flat.

Teresa looked horrified, not sure if she should run after her daughter or stay to hear what I had to say. I wasn't sure what I should do either.

I looked over at Grant who appeared to be regretting his words. But he didn't know. I knew they all thought we invited them to Christmas at our place for a celebratory reason.

"Uh—" I began, slowly standing up. But that wasn't a great decision as my legs shook beneath me.

"Leo, you guys are scaring us. What is it?" Diane asked, being close enough to see my body's constant movement despite my best efforts to keep it still.

"Natalie has brain cancer—"

The sound of a thud woke me. Or what felt like a wake-up anyway.

"Ow, fuck," I heard Grant say.

The door to the room I was in opened as I sat up. Natalie's present rolling from my chest to the floor.

"Glad to see you're still alive," he said like he had meant to come in there.

And maybe he had.

"Are you drunk?" I asked, getting to my feet.

"Depends what you consider drunk," he said with a smirk.

He *was* drunk. But who was I to judge? As Mom said, he had been through a lot. Although you didn't see me shit-faced at Christmas.

"Sounds an awful lot like judging."

The sound of Natalie's voice made my attention go to her present. Grant eyed it too.

"Who's the small box for?" he asked, more than likely innocently. But with his current state I wasn't sure.

"No one," I answered as I picked it up off the ground.

He exhaled as his eyes rolled almost out of his head. "Fuck, you bought a gift for your dead wife?" he exclaimed. "You're more fucking delusional than I thought."

"Come off it. I'm not fucking delusional."

"What in the Sam Hill is going on in here?" Dad asked as he stepped into the doorway only a few feet from Grant. "Are you drunk?" he asked him, wrinkling his nose.

"I think you should be a little less worried about my drinking and a little more worried about your older kid."

"What's he talking about, Leo?" I heard my mom say, though I couldn't see her until my dad stepped aside.

They all stood there in the guest room staring at me. The looks they were giving me were almost as torturous as reliving my life with Natalie day by day. They were scared, and that time, they weren't hiding it.

"He bought Natalie a present," Grant finally answered for me.

"Oh, Leo," my mom said, her tone oozing sympathy.

"I'm not crazy. I know she's dead," I said.

They saw me wince. I didn't even realize the pain had been physical until they seemed to feel it too.

"Then why did you buy her a present?" Grant asked.

"Did you buy it before she died?" my mom asked wishfully.

"Does it matter?" I asked.

"It would tell us if you're crazy or not."

"Grant!" my mom exclaimed.

"Well, it would," he replied.

I looked at my dad who had yet to say anything. "I'm not crazy," I reiterated, my voice calm and even-keeled, despite my insides feeling the exact opposite.

My dad nodded before speaking softly. "You're in denial."

My hands shook as I clutched the box in them.

I *had* been in denial. I had been holding on to the hope that it was all just a nightmare that I would wake up from.

Their eyes on me were a loud alarm. It *was* time to wake up. And instead of her being there and it all having been a dream, it turned out my life *was* a nightmare. And the reality of her death being real was something I could no longer deny.

Chapter Five

{Wednesday, January 10ᵗʰ, 2018}

"Sorry you couldn't make it out for New Year's," Mark said as he took a sip of his drink.

I shrugged. "Wasn't that I couldn't; I just didn't want to."

"I see you've entered the angry phase as the therapist said you would."

I rolled my eyes at Natalie's words. I had done the same to the therapist in the one and only session I had with him.

Mark ignored my comment as he was known to do.

"What kind of trouble you looking to get into tonight?" he asked.

"Trouble? Since when do I know how to get into trouble?"

"Oh, come on. We used to stir up some shit. What about starting with some tequila? That always helped you loosen up."

"And by 'loosen up,' you mean vomiting up all my insides."

He slapped his hand between my shoulder blades. "Yeah, I guess you never were good at holdin' your own."

"Just with tequila."

"And gin."

I rolled my eyes again. If I was going to enjoy myself, I was going to need to drown out my wife's voice.

"Let's do some Fireball," Mark exclaimed.

I shrugged. "Whatever gets the job done."

He raised his brow.

"I mean, whatever gets me drunk."

His smile grew. "That's the spirit! Two rounds of Fireball comin'' up," he said before he disappeared into the crowd.

"Pass it back here," Natalie said, taking the fifth of whiskey from Oliver in the front seat of the car.

I watched as she unscrewed the cap, tipped it back, and drank it as if the whiskey was water.

"You should probably take it easy," I said as she put it back down and glanced at me.

Her eyes were bloodshot and completely glossed over. Although they had already been that way when I had picked her up earlier that night. She said she had pre-gamed. But I hadn't really taken Natalie as a drinker, let alone someone who pre-gamed a night of drinking.

"Are you okay?" I asked when she had looked away but had yet to put the bottle down.

"I'm fine. Can't a girl have a little fun?"

"Of course, but you're pretty wasted."

"Maybe you're just not wasted enough*," she replied as she put the bottle to my mouth and tried to force me to drink.*

"Natalie, stop," I said as some trickled down my neck and onto my shirt.

"Shit, I'm sorry," she replied. It wasn't for the way she was acting, but because of the small amount of whiskey I was wearing. "Let's get you cleaned up," she said as she started to pull at my shirt from the bottom.

"Come on, Nat, knock it off," I said softly.

"Oh, don't act like you don't want to get naked with me," she replied as she moved to straddle me in the backseat of the car while her friend continued driving us back to her place.

"I mean, of course I do, but not like this."

I glanced at Oliver in the passenger seat who looked like he wanted to be sympathetic but also seemed jealous. They were going to be no help.

Natalie started kissing my neck. My mind and my body felt like they were being ripped in opposite directions. Why was she acting like this?

She moved her hand down to my jeans and rubbed against them. "See, you like me drunk," she said with a mischievous smile.

"Nat, this isn't like you," I said as she went back to kissing my neck.

But her lips left my skin when what I said had registered. "How the fuck would you know what I'm like? You've known me, what, four months?"

Her eyes were glossed from the booze, but as she looked at me, it was almost like she had shifted and was going to cry.

"What are you talking about, Nat? Of course I know you."

"No, you don't," she replied, moving off of me. "You're like every other guy out there. Once you fuck me, you're just going to leave."

Where was this coming from? How could she think that about me? Four months wasn't a long time in the grand scheme of life, but to me it felt like an eternity.

"Nat, I would never leave you, I—"

"—Don't," she said.

"Don't what?"

"Don't you dare say you love me."

Was that what I was about to say? I mean I did. But why didn't she want me to say it?

"Natalie, we're at your house," Desy said from the driver's seat.

My eyes stayed fixated on Natalie, my expression completely twisted in my confused state.

Natalie pulled on the handle and opened the door.

I opened mine too.

"Don't," she said again.

Don't what? But she continued before I could ask. "Don't walk me to my door. Just fucking leave."

The door slammed shut.

"Wait for me, okay?" I asked Desy, who nodded her head.

I shut the door and followed behind as Natalie stumbled to her house.

"Shots, shots, shots, shots—" Mark sang to himself as he set the glasses down in front of us.

"Alright, my man, bad decision making starts here," he exclaimed.

Why he was aiming to make bad decisions I wasn't sure. But for years he had had my back. If I drank, he drank. If I cried, he cried. If I started a fight, he finished it. Mark had been my ride or die best friend. Well, until he wasn't.

"To old friendships," he said as he raised one of the glasses.

I raised mine too and then tipped it back.

It burned, but I was fine with that. I actually was craving something a little stronger. Something that would do a little more damage.

"How'd Christmas back home go?" he asked, pushing the next shot towards me.

"It went."

"Beth said your mom made you see a shrink."

I glanced over at him and picked up the glass.

"And what? Beth talks to my mom now?"

"Oh, come on, you know Beth loved talking with your mom."

"Yeah, years ago. Why's she suddenly talking to her again?" I asked. "Better yet, why are *you* talking to me again?"

"We already talked about this," he replied, his brows furrowing. "Shit happens. People get busy. Now come on, let's drink!" he continued as he tossed back the second shot. So I did the same. "So the shrink—did it help?"

I narrowed my eyes at him. "Do you think I'd be here drinking with you if it did?"

"Fair. So, what'd you do that made your mom make you go there?"

"I bought Nat a present."

"Ah, yeah," he replied as his eyes went wide. "I could see a problem with that."

I shook my head. "And she didn't make me go. I went so she wouldn't worry."

"Should she?"

"What?"

"Worry?"

"No. I mean, it wasn't like I was expecting Natalie to rise from the dead. I just thought it was possible that I was in a coma or something. Or like this was just a long ass nightmare or something."

He nodded. "And the shrink didn't help?"

"No—I don't know. He said that, for it to help, I have to want help first."

"Sounds reasonable. So, do you want help?"

"No, what I want is to get shit-faced and finally get some fucking sleep."

"Now *that,* my friend, is something I can help with," he said before taking off back to the bar.

Natalie stumbled as she walked up her deck. I put my arms out to help her.

"Don't fucking touch me," she yelled.

I swallowed a lump in my throat, glancing briefly back at Desy and Oliver in the car.

What had I done? Why was she being like that?

Before her keys could find the lock, the light above it went on and the door opened.

"Jesus Christ, Natalie," Teresa said exasperatedly.

"What? I'm allowed to drink!"

"Drink, yes. Drain the whole liquor cabinet, no."

"It's not like you leave a whole lot in there," Natalie retorted and then laughed.

Teresa looked at me, her eyes sympathetic for a moment.

"Thanks for bringing her home," she said to me. "You haven't been drinking, have you?"

"Uh, I've had a little," I said, but then pointed to the car. "But Desy hasn't, and she drove."

Teresa nodded as she moved out of the way so Natalie could enter the house.

"Do you want to say bye to your boyfriend?" she yelled to Natalie who had disappeared inside.

"What's the point? He's going to break up with me anyway."

Teresa's eyes widened, but so did mine.

"What's she talking about?" she asked me.

"I don't know. She's been acting really weird all night and she keeps saying I'm going to leave her…"

Teresa rolled her eyes, but it didn't seem to be at me.

She pulled the door closed and we stood on the porch.

"We got served with paperwork earlier today saying that her dad wants to terminate his parental rights."

"She's seventeen," I replied, my eyes shifting to the ground and then back to her. "Why do that now?"

"Apparently, the woman he has been seeing just gave birth to his little girl."

"What does that have to do with Natalie?"

She sighed and put her arms over her chest. "He wanted a clean slate. No ties to his old life. And apparently, that meant with his daughter too."

***

"Sweet Caroline—ba, ba, ba—" Mark sang into the microphone as the bar cheered him on and sang along.

I envied the ease of his life. There was a time where he would have said the same about mine. Well, where he *did*say the same. But I never understood that. Because our lives, for all intents and purposes, were equal. Good jobs, married—sometimes happily, sometimes not, but a good solid structure on the foundation we had built for ourselves.

My eyelids drooped as I finished off the last of my sixth whiskey and Coke. I knew, when I stood up, there was a chance gravity wouldn't be my friend. But Mark was always willing to be there to keep me steady. To get me home. He always had my back.

"Jesus Christ, you're shit-faced," Mark said as he sat on the kitchen counter.

I, on the other hand, was sitting on the floor, laughing at anything and everything happening at the party.

"Who knew you just needed the wifey to disappear for the weekend for you to let loose?"

"She's not my wife," I replied with no real inflection.

"Not yet anyway," he retorted.

"That's correct," I said, pointing my finger up at him. "But someday."

He laughed; then I did too. I loved the thought of making her my wife. I wished someday was sooner. But I had only just bought the ring a month before in Mexico. I was waiting for the perfect time to ask.

"Do you want to play another round of waterfall?" Mark asked, jumping down from the counter.

"Do I seem like I should play another round?"

He shook his head. "Probably not. Goddamn lightweight."

I shrugged.

"Well, you can at least come watch me play so I can keep an eye on you. Make sure you don't choke on your own vomit."

"Vomit? Who's vomiting?"

"Probably you in like five minutes."

I didn't question it. I probably would be.

"You're a good friend," I said to him, and he leaned down and put his arm under my shoulder to lift me up.

"That, and well, the future Mrs. would kill me if I let anything happen to you."

"That she would."

Once he had me to my feet, I felt the room spin.

"The five minutes might be up," I said with a grimace.

"Oh, goody," he joked. "Let's get you to the toilet."

He all but carried me to the bathroom and shut the door.

"Alright now, aim into the bowl. I don't think Kevin wants to clean up puke before class in the morning."

"That's so sweet of you to care about Kevin," I mocked.

"Kevin's a douche, but no one should have to clean up your vomit. Especially with the shit you eat."

I laughed, but as soon as I did, the contents of my stomach came too. Luckily, I made it into the bowl.

"Remind me again why I take you drinking?" Mark asked as he stood on the other side of the bathroom.

I didn't—or rather couldn't—respond.

"Just kidding. Although, if you puke in our room when we get back, I may have to reconsider our friendship."

He seemed to be having a conversation with himself. Maybe he was drunk too. I could never tell in comparison to myself.

"Shit, it's the cops," someone yelled from outside the bathroom door.

"Ah, fuck," he stated.

"Shit," I groaned quietly as I rested my head on the bathroom floor.

"No, no, no—" Mark said as he moved towards me. "No time to rest. We have to get out of here."

I exhaled but didn't move. "I don't know if I can."

"Well, you have to. I can't have you getting kicked out of school. Or a minor in possession charge or whatever the fuck they do to us underaged assholes."

He lifted my arm and tucked his around me again, lifting me against my will. My stomach felt like it was trying to stay on the floor where I had been.

The music was still playing. We didn't know what was going on, and only Mark cared. I just wanted to sit by the toilet and continue to revisit the chili dogs I had had for dinner.

He walked me to the door, opened it, and peered around the corner.

"Shit," he said and then pulled us back before slamming the door and locking it.

"Hey!" someone yelled from the other side.

"They spotted me," he whispered.

"You gotta come out, son," the officer said through the bathroom door.

Mark looked at the window. There was no way I was jumping out of anything, even though we were on the main floor.

"If you don't come out, I will come in," the officer threatened.

"Jesus, he's really willing to break down a door just to bust a kid?" I asked.

"Shhh—" Mark replied, trying to think.

"Just jump out the window," I said as I fought my eyes to stay open. "No point in us both getting in trouble."

"True," he said.

"Kid, I'm serious, you have thirty seconds to get out here, or I'm going to get you for resisting arrest as well."

He lowered me down, but as I waited to touch the floor, I got the edge of the tub instead.

"Get in here," he said, all but pushing me in.

"Why?"

"Just shut up," he said, and then pulled the curtain shut.

"Don't say a fuckin' word," he whispered once more.

"Mark—"

I watched through the crack in the curtain as Mark opened the door.

"Hold your pants on. I just had to take a piss," he said to the cop just before I saw him jerked out of the doorway.

"You have the right to remain silent, anything you say or do.."

Mark put his arm around my shoulder. "You gonna join in on the fun?"

I looked at the stage he had just left. It had been years since I had done karaoke. I didn't mind the attention, and I didn't care about my terrible voice. It had always just been something I did with Mark. And when he took off, I didn't have a best friend to do that with anymore.

Natalie never took it personally. At least she always said she didn't. She never got my relationship with Mark, but she respected it. She knew it was something she didn't have to understand, because he was my best friend, not hers.

"Ignoring me won't make me go away," he joked.

I downed one of the shots still on the table and looked at him. "Alright, let's do this."

"There he is!" he exclaimed with excitement in his eyes. "Fuck yeah!"

I followed him up to the stage.

"Y'all asked for an encore," he said, though I was sure they hadn't. "And for this one, I'm bringing my best bud."

He said something to the person in charge of the music and handed me a microphone.

A smile crossed my face the moment I heard the clapping come over the speaker.

"Ladies and gentlemen," Mark said into the microphone as he glanced over at me. "This is 'Mambo No. 5.'"

I chuckled for the first time in weeks, maybe months. It felt good to let something other than anger or sadness show through.

I had forgotten how much I loved my time with Mark. He wasn't the usual friendship I kept, and people rarely saw the good in him that I was able to see. But I knew him better. It was why it had hurt so bad when he left.

But things had just started to get better with Natalie and me, so I focused all my energy on her and our marriage, instead of going to him to figure out what had happened. Maybe it was as he said— people grew apart. I hadn't sensed it, but I had been missing a lot of things back then. Maybe I was trapped in my tunnel vision not only with Natalie, but with Mark too.

"Should we call Mark and Beth?" I asked Natalie as we walked into the living room with our dessert of popcorn and chocolate covered raisins.

She took her seat and looked for the remote before answering.

"I'm sure they've heard by now," she replied, popping one of the raisins into her mouth.

84

"No way. They would've called."

"I don't know. It's been a few years. Maybe they don't want to call."

"But for this? You think they wouldn't call to at least—" I froze.

"—say goodbye?" she finished.

I nodded, choked up on the words I had so casually tried to say.

She sighed. "I think that, if they want to say goodbye, then they will. I don't want to feel like I'm forcing anyone to come visit."

"You're not forcing anyone," I replied.

"I know, but I'm just saying I don't want to spend whatever time I have left surrounded by people wanting to make amends with me before I kick the bucket."

I took the seat beside her, but I knew she could feel the tension in my body from her words.

"Sorry, I know you hate my cavalier attitude. But listen, I want to spend all my time with you, my mom, and Diane. Everyone else had their chance to be a part of my life. And if they aren't one of those people I just named, then they'll just have to see me on the other side."

"Noted."

I shifted back on the couch as she turned on the TV. I put my arm around her, while she nestled herself to my side and rested her head on my shoulder.

"Where'd you go up there?" Mark asked as we left the stage.

"What do you mean?"

I took my seat back at the table as Mark signaled to the waitress for another round.

"Your mouth was moving, but you were like, I don't know, spaced out."

"You mean drunk?" I asked with a laugh.

He chuckled, but it seemed forced. "Nah, it was like you weren't here."

My brows furrowed. "I guess I'm not the only one who's wasted," I said as the waitress set down the drinks and I picked mine up. "To old friendships," I repeated from his earlier toast.

He picked his up. "To rekindled friendships," he added.

***

"You could have totally gotten that girl's number," Mark said as he put his arm under me like old times, helping me stumble away from the bar.

"Probably," I replied with a chuckle. "But I didn't *want* that girl's number."

"All in good time, my friend."

"No, I'm never dating again."

He laughed. "Yeah, okay."

"What's the point?" I asked, swaying a little away from him as he pulled me back in.

"What's the point? I don't know—sex, love, marriage, kids. Some of that or all of it."

"But why? All that does is lead to heartbreak."

"Oh, God, you're not going to start singing country, are you?"

"Fuck off," I replied, trying to push at his face, but missing. "I'm just saying. No one will ever be as perfect as Natalie."

"I agree."

"So, what's the point?"

"The point is, you're thirty-two, have a good job, and don't look half bad. And well, it would be a crime to waste what you have to offer."

"Which is?"

He side-eyed me. "You're a good man, Leo Algar. Much better than all of us shitheads out here."

"Shitheads? There are multiple? I thought there was only you."

He sat me down on a bench as he pulled out his phone. "Nah, I'm just King Shithead. There are many more of us."

"Where are we going?" I asked, looking around as I ignored his comment.

He put his phone to his ear. "Well, apparently the wait for an Uber is about forty minutes. And since I don't need you freezing to death on my watch, I'm calling my wife."

"Ooooh, she's going to hate you," I said with a chuckle.

"Yeah, probably. But she'll do it for you."

"For me?"

"I'm King of Shitheads, remember? Ain't nobody doin' shit for me. But, for you, my friend—these women would move the goddamn earth."

Chapter Six
{Wednesday, February 14ᵗʰ, 2018}

"As you enter there would be an Allee, like seen here in the picture," I said, clicking to the next slide. "And that would open up to a Bosque at the end—"

"Leo, let me stop you there," the client, Robert, said as he put his hand up.

I exhaled but put on the same smile I had given him the last two meetings he had stopped the same way.

"What is it, Robert?" Wayne asked, sensing I probably wasn't the best person to be talking at that moment.

"I don't know," he said with a sigh. "I mean, I like it like the other two ideas. It's just—I don't know—it's just not, *it*. Ya know?" he asked, looking from Wayne to me.

"No, we don't know. This is exactly—"

"—We know what you're saying, Robert," Wayne interrupted me as he stood up from his seat. "It just doesn't have the wow factor you're looking for."

My eyes shot to Wayne.

No *wow* factor? The fuck was the guy expecting?

"Exactly," Robert said, then turned his attention back to me. "It's not that you didn't do an excellent job. All of these designs are perfect."

My brows furrowed.

If they were *perfect,* why wasn't he using them?

"Just not perfect for *you*," I stated, the smile long gone from my face.

Robert's grin faded. "Listen, this is nothing against you. It has to be difficult to have your head really in your work after a loss like yours."

"This has nothing to do with my work, or where my head is at. You've changed your mind three times now."

Robert looked a little caught off guard by my tone. Wayne's eyes didn't seem to hold the same shock.

"Leo, why don't you wait for me in my office," Wayne said calmly.

"You know," I continued to Robert, "I've busted my ass on these designs for weeks, getting them to your exact wants and needs, and then you tell me they aren't right because of my dead wife?"

"Leo," Wayne tried to interject.

"I mean it's a fucking insurance company for Christ's sake, not Dodger Stadium."

"My office. Now," Wayne said, his tone more stern than I had ever heard it.

I grabbed my portfolio off the desk and walked out the door.

The decorations in the hallway whipped aside as I breezed by them. I was seeing red, and it wasn't just from the sea of hearts that signified Valentine's Day was upon us.

My blood boiled inside of me, as the few people heading my way got out of it quickly.

Before I arrived at Wayne's office, I hit the teddy bear cutout that sat on a small table just outside of it. Petty, I know, but for a second it made me feel just a tiny bit better.

Natalie shrieked with excitement as she held the teddy bear tightly to her chest.

"I love it," she said, her eyes looking lovingly into mine.

"I'm glad," I replied as I kissed her forehead. "Also, I know you're not big on chocolate, so I got two bags of gummy bears."

Her eyes widened. "These are a stomachache waiting to happen."

"Well, don't eat them all in one sitting and you should be okay."

She sat back on the couch and ripped open the bag. "Don't you know by now that I have no self-control when it comes to sweets?"

I smiled as she tossed a few into her mouth.

"Yeah, I have seen a theme developing there," I replied.

She set the bag down on the side table and moved her body over to mine.

"Do you want your present?" she asked, her tone shifting from excitement to mysterious.

"Absolutely," I replied. "Your gifts are pretty epic."

"Epic?" she asked with a laugh.

"I mean, my birthday gift was the best gift I've ever gotten."

"That's because you haven't gotten this one yet."

I heard Wayne pick up the cardboard bear from outside his office. After a moment, he stepped in and shut his door.

"That was bullshit, Wayne, and you know it," I said the minute the door latched.

"Sit down," he said calmly, but I just kept pacing.

"I mean, who says that shit? Who the fuck is he—"

"—The client, that's who!" Wayne replied loudly. "Now sit!"

That time I complied.

He inhaled, and then exhaled, choosing his next words carefully. "I think you should take more time off."

I shot up from my chair once more, all but leaping towards his desk. "Because that asshole can't make up his mind?"

"No, because you can't control yourself in front of clients."

"Jesus, you make me sound like a fucking lunatic. If they would stop saying shit about my dead wife, I would stop responding in the manner I do."

"They're being sympathetic. You're just too deep in the thick of it to see people's good intentions."

"Good intentions?" I tipped my head back and laughed. "They don't have good intentions when they say that shit! They are looking for an excuse to not pay us for our fucking time. I designed every fucking thing he asked," I said, slamming my portfolio down in front of Wayne at his desk. "I designed it to every specification that he said it needed to include. But he has the audacity to say my head isn't in it."

"Can you tell me it *is*?"

I glared at Wayne. "Are you fucking kidding me?" I flipped open the portfolio to the newest page and jammed my pointer finger into it. "Is that not my head being in the game, Wayne? I've hit every deadline, been at every meeting, I've been pulling all-nighters—"

"—You're right. You are doing all of those things—"

"—Then what's the problem?"

He shook his head. "You're unorganized. You're moody. You can't even speak to the clients without being an asshole, let alone your co-workers. You reek of booze multiple times a week." He paused. "Need I go on?"

I pushed myself off from where I had been leaning over his desk, but I didn't know what to say.

"Listen, Leo," he began again with a sigh. "When Mary-Ann died—"

"—Don't," I said.

"Don't what? Don't say I understand? Is it such a bad thing that someone can relate?"

I shook my head, but it wasn't in response to what he had said; it was more to myself to stop the tears that were forming.

"Leo, you need more time. This is just a part of the grieving process. You're angry and hurt, and it's understandable. But what kind of boss would I be if I let you blow up your career when you don't need to?"

I walked to the door.

"It'll pass, Leo," he said as I paused with my hand on the knob. "I know it doesn't feel like it, but the anger you have—that pain in your chest—it won't be there forever."

***

On the drive back to my house, I tried to concentrate on something other than Robert and the bullshit leave I was being forced to take. My anger had subsided a little after packing up some of my things and leaving, but it was towing the line of which way it was going to go.

Natalie pulled my hand as she led me up the stairs. The teddy bear I had given her was held tightly in the other.

Teresa was out for the night. Her first date since her husband had split. I was excited to be alone with Natalie. But the more time we got like that, the more I wasn't sure we were going to be able to control ourselves.

"My present is in your room?" I asked, playing coy.

I assumed the present was alone time with her, in her bed. And hey, even if it wasn't sex, I was game for whatever that entailed.

"It is," she said, opening her door.

"Wow, did you clean it just for me?"

She punched my arm playfully. "It's not like it was that bad."

"Ah, babe, there are many things I love about you, but your sense of tidiness isn't one of them."

Her eyes met mine.

I had said it.

The words made her smile.

"There are many things I love about you too," she replied.

She led me into her room and shut the door. We had never had the door shut before. We had always needed to listen for her mom coming up the stairs.

"Shit, saying I love you gets a closed door?"

She smirked. "Saying I love you doesn't get shit," she said as she walked over to her window and closed the curtains. "But meaning it—well—that gets you everything."

She turned back towards me and her eyes softened.

Natalie was a complicated girl. She had such a confident, daring exterior. But she was her most beautiful when she was vulnerable. When she let me see the side of her she was scared of. The side that was scared of being hurt like her dad had hurt her. Like her dad had hurt her mom. The side that needed me. I loved that I could take all her fears away.

"You're so beautiful," I whispered, but it was loud enough for her to hear and make her smile.

"You're not too shabby yourself," she replied. "Are you ready for your present?"

I nodded, trying my best to not show how eager I was.

She laughed.

I think it showed anyway.

She unbuttoned her blouse, the silk from whatever was under it revealed a small part of itself.

"I went with Desy to Victoria's Secret this weekend and got your present," she began.

"Ah, Vicki's secret," I replied, nodding my head. "Ya know, I think my body type just wasn't made to rock their lingerie."

She smirked as she shimmied her pants to the ground.

94

"But clearly yours was," I said, not being able to take my eyes off of her.

"So you like it?"

I reminded myself to blink. *"I don't think I've ever liked anything more."*

She lifted a brow. *"So, suddenly reading on the football field is chopped liver?"* she asked, putting her hands on her hips.

"We've read on the football field?" I asked and then jumped up from the bed laughing as I wrapped my arms around her. *"I'm kidding,"* I continued, looking down into her eyes. *"But I do love it."*

"As much as you love me?"

"I could never love anything as much as I love you."

A loud popping noise followed by the sudden jerk of my wheel stole me from the moment I'd been reliving.

I gripped the wheel, feeling the pull to the right, trying to keep it straight.

I let off the accelerator and clicked on my hazards as I rolled to a stop.

"Fuck!" I yelled.

"Calm down; it's just a flat."

"Calm down? I went off on a client. My boss thinks I've lost my fucking mind and put me on leave. My tire just blew. And now I'm sitting on the side of the fucking road talking to my dead wife."

I waited for a response, but the car was silent.

"Fuck!" I yelled again, as I slammed my hand on the wheel.

I knew I should control my breathing. I knew I needed to remain calm, go into the back, grab the spare, and change it. But my chest hurt, my eyes burned, and every moment I was awake I couldn't feel anything but anger.

I exhaled and opened my door. I walked to the trunk and opened it. After shifting random junk around, I was able to see the opening to the spare. I pulled it up, and as my day would have it, it was empty.

Before I knew it, I was smiling. Then laughing.

Cool, I *had* fucking lost it.

I ran my hand through my hair as I slammed the trunk shut and pulled out my phone.

Leo: Blew a tire. Can you pick me up?
Mark: Sure thing. Where you at?

I texted him my location and got back into my car.

Resting my forehead on the steering wheel, I closed my eyes, trying like hell to make the boulder in my chest move just slightly so I could breathe even a little easier. But it didn't budge. No amount of breathing or eye-shutting was going to lift the anger or carry away the pain. I was stuck in it.

"No, I'm just on my way home," I said to Mark who was on speaker phone in my car. *"Wayne's been riding me all week about this deadline, so I figured I'd knock it out a day early. At least tomorrow should be better."*

"Wait? You're not home yet?"

"No—are you even listening?" I asked with a laugh.

"Yeah, just curious when your 'oh-shit' tone is going to sink in."

"My oh-shit tone?"

He sighed. "Leo, my man, you stepped in it this time."

He couldn't see me, but the silence gave away my confusion.

"What's the date of your deadline?" he asked.

"The fifteenth."

"Right. Meaning today would be?"

"Oh, shit."

"Precisely," he said, then chuckled.

"Then why aren't you with Beth? Why are you talking to me?"

"Well," he began with another laugh. "See, being the great husband that I am, I left work early today. Made her dinner, made a bath for the two of us, gave her a bracelet she's been eyeing for months, and then fucked—"

"—Okay, I got it."

"I would have never guessed your marriage would end before mine," he continued in a playful tone.

"Shut up. It's only Valentine's Day. Natalie doesn't give a shit about Hallmark bullshit."

"That's what they say, but they all want to be shown that someone gives a shit. Even if it's for a made-up day."

I sighed. "Well, Natalie knows I love her, and she knows work's been stressful."

"I'm just giving you shit, man. I'm sure Natalie will be fine."

I glanced at a gas station as I passed it. "I'll call you tomorrow, okay?"

"Yup, good luck," he said before clicking off the phone.

There was a knock at the window that caused my head to burrow into the horn, pulling attention to my car.

Mark laughed from the other side of the glass. "Getting some shut eye?" he asked as I opened the door.

"That would be a nice change of pace."

I grabbed my stuff out of my car and locked it.

"Didn't you and Nat have Triple A?"

"She did on her car. I didn't need it on mine. I didn't mind changing a flat."

"What changed?" he asked as we got into his car.

"No spare."

"Oh, yeah, that makes it difficult. Where'd it go?"

"Nat and I had to use it when we took a small road trip last summer."

"And you didn't replace it?"

I looked over at him. "I was a little busy with my wife dying and all."

He went silent.

I shouldn't have been talking. It was getting me into all sorts of trouble. The not-giving-a-shit, no filter was a terrible way to live. Yet it seemed to be the only thing I knew how to do.

"You need a drink," Mark said.

"That didn't sound like a question."

"Because it wasn't. There's a bar a few streets over. We'll stop there."

I didn't say no. Though I was sure that wouldn't have mattered. He hadn't given me any time to say no. He just flipped on his blinker and took a hard left.

"Nat?" I asked as I opened our front door with a gas station rose and what was left of the Valentine candy in my hand.

There was no response.

The light was on in the living room, but she wasn't there.

There was a faint smell of chicken and some kind of spice in the air.

Shit. Had she cooked?

I walked into the kitchen. Pots and pans were piled in the sink, the counter was a mess, and the dining room table had a meal for two that hadn't been touched.

I ran my hand over my forehead and then glanced at the clock on the stove. It was a little past 9. It was early for bed.

A red spot on the floor caught my eye. I grabbed a napkin and wiped it. It was blood.

Fuck. She had cut herself cooking dinner for me. A dinner I had missed because of work. A dinner she had made to surprise me. And all I had brought was pain, chocolate she didn't even like, and a slightly withering rose.

"It's not our typical scene, but it has booze, and judging from your silence, I assume that's just what you need."

I looked over at Mark and attempted a grin and failed

We opened our doors and went inside anyway.

"Two shots of Jack," Mark said to the bartender as we took the two open stools.

He nodded and walked away.

"So, besides the whole dead wife thing, what's eatin' you?"

I ran my hand through my hair and glanced around the bar.

He wasn't kidding. It really wasn't our scene. The crowd was at least ten years younger. Some looked like they were more than likely sporting fake IDs.

"Where did you bring me?"

"There's a college campus nearby."

"Keeping tabs on local campus bars? Does Beth know about your extracurricular activities?" I asked as our shots were set in front of us.

"Thanks," he replied to the bartender before he looked over at me. "Actually, I was scouting some real estate last week—"

"—Is that what they're calling it now?"

He rolled his eyes. "I was looking at a spot for our new office, asshole."

I chuckled. It was brief but nice.

"So are you going to talk?" he asked.

"About?"

His brows furrowed. "You're trying awfully hard to avoid answering."

"You're trying awfully hard to get me to answer."

"Fair," he conceded. "But if I go home with nothing to report to Beth, she will just sic me on you again."

I shook my head. "Do I at least get to drink first?"

"Oh, absolutely." He picked up the shot and raised it into the air, motioning for me to do the same.

"Do we have to make a toast every time we drink?" I asked.

He laughed. "To no toasts, only drinks, tonight."

***

"I'll be right back," I said to Mark as I stood up to head to the bathroom.

He grabbed my arm, causing me to look his way.

"You good?" he asked as he laughed.

The two of him I saw for a minute merged together, as I placed my hand on his shoulder.

"I'm golden, no worries—just gotta take a leak," I replied.

He let go of my arm as I took a breath and began my walk to the restroom.

I stumbled down the back hall, trying to keep my balance.

Thoughts of my past that I had been hoping to drown out with liquor seemed to push through with ease as the hallway in the bar turned into my upstairs hallway at home.

I rested my hand on the wall, blinking a few times. I could hear the crowd from the bar, but when I looked around, it was only me and my house. I leaned my back up against the wall, succumbing to the memory of a night I had longed to forget.

As I walked down the hall, withering rose in one hand, candy in the other, I saw another spot of red on the floor.

I stopped in front of the bathroom and pushed on the partially open door. "Nat?"

I glanced around the bathroom, but she wasn't there. But she had been. The light was on. There were a few more spots of blood and a couple bunched up towels.

Maybe she had cut herself worse than I thought and took herself to the hospital. Wouldn't she have called?

I reached into my pocket and looked at my cell. No missed calls. No missed texts.

I clicked her name, listening to the ring coming from my phone, but then hearing it from the other room.

I walked to the bedroom. The door was open, but the light was off.

Her phone screen was lit up on the nightstand, but there was no movement from the bed.

"Nat?" I asked, setting the rose, the teddy and my phone on the dresser.

The lump in the bed covered by our down comforter didn't move.

I walked over to the bed and climbed in next to her.

"Nat?"

She turned her head slightly, the moon light shining in and reflecting in her eyes.

Her expression was hollow.

"I'm sorry, babe," I began. "I completely spaced."

A tear fell from the corner of her eye and got lost in her hair.

I lowered my head to hers. "I'm such a dick. I swear I didn't even realize what day it was. I was so caught up in the deadline—"

Her eyes flooded with tears, but she didn't make a sound.

"The dinner looked amazing, I'm sure we can just warm it up," I continued, giving her my best attempt at a smile.

She shut her eyes.

Everything I was saying was making it worse. "Nat, please say something."

She exhaled, her breath shaky. "I'm sorry," she said.

My brows furrowed. Out of all the things she could have said, apologizing was not one that I had expected.

"For what?" I asked, with a slight chuckle.

"I wanted to surprise you—" she said softly.

I kissed her forehead. "You did surprise me. I'm just an idiot and showed up late."

"—I got dressed in the new lingerie I bought. I cooked dinner for us—"

"God, I'm so sorry I missed that," I interrupted, thinking of my beautiful wife cooking for me in some sexy lingerie. I had really fucked up.

"—But then there was blood."

"I saw that. Did you cut yourself? You try so hard to be Gordon Ramsay sometimes," I joked.

Her body tensed up as her eyes met mine.

"It hurt so bad. I didn't know what to do. I was so scared."

My expression fell. "Did you bandage it up? How deep was it?" I asked, as I began to move the blankets to get to her hand.

"I thought I was overreacting," she continued without moving.

Her tone was so soft.

Why was she speaking so softly? She didn't sound angry. She didn't really sound sad either. She just sounded different.

"Nat, let me look at it."

"I wanted to surprise you," she said again.

"I know, you said that. And I'm sorry," I responded sincerely.

"You would have made a great dad," she continued, her tone shifted just long enough to clear her throat.

"Wait, what are you talking about?"

"I kept thinking about what they would look like. How you would look when you held them. I had bought a gender-neutral onesie."

I shifted up in bed, but she still didn't move.

"Nat, what are you talking about?" I persisted.

Her eyes found mine once more. "I'm sorry," she said again.

I stared at her for a moment, not knowing what to say. Needing more time for it to register. "You were pregnant?" I asked.

She nodded as a few more tears rolled down her face. "But I'm not anymore."

"Are you okay?" I heard a woman's voice ask.

I glanced up at her, though I wasn't exactly sure when I had ended up on the floor.

Tears covered my face, so I wiped them away and then nodded.

Her brows furrowed. "Are you sure? You're bleeding."

I looked at my hand, seeing blood smeared across it. My eyes grew wide as I searched my brain for what had happened. How I had ended up bleeding. Or whose blood it was that was on me.

"It's coming from your nose," she said, growing concerned at my confused state of mind.

I wiped my hand under it, and more blood appeared.

"Is someone here with you? I can go get them."

I shook my head, though speaking would have made my response more convincing. But I wasn't certain that was an option at the moment.

My chest felt heavy, painful, somehow on fire, though there was no smoke billowing from it.

I pushed myself up to my feet, my shoulder crashing into the wall as I attempted to balance myself.

I was certain she said something else or asked again if she should get someone. But I was concentrating on the fast-paced rhythm of my heartbeat, and my shaking hands.

The door to the bathroom swung shut behind me as I made my way to the sink. I turned on the water, resting my hands on the rim. I glanced up, seeing a drip of blood leave my nose and fall into the pooling water below.

I closed the door to the bedroom enough so that the light from the hallway didn't shine in but left it open so I could hear Natalie if she needed me.

The pain from finding her earlier that night in a state of shock hadn't left my chest. I had yet to cry, to scream, to feel any emotion past that because I needed to be strong—for Natalie.

I walked to the bathroom and picked up the towels to put into the wash and cleaned up the few dried blood spots on the floor.

The doctor said she miscarried. She was eleven weeks along. Apparently, she had known for a few weeks now. She was going to tell me that night.

I walked downstairs and into the kitchen where dinner was still laid out on the table.

I grabbed the garbage container and unloaded the nicely plated meals into it.

As I put my plate back down, I looked at the gift-wrapped box next to it. I sighed, taking a seat where I should have been hours before.

The box was light and beautifully wrapped. I was certain she had watched a YouTube tutorial. The woman couldn't wrap to save her life.

I pulled on the bow, and took the top off the box, peering inside at what my wife had planned for our special evening.

The tears that had been pressing against the back of my eyes showed themselves, falling down my cheek and onto my wrinkled button-up that more than likely now smelled like hospital and bad coffee.

Setting the lid to the box on the table, I pulled out the pregnancy test with a sticky note attached to it.

"I sanitized it, so please don't throw it away. It's a keepsake."

I smiled through the tears. But that just made more fall.

I reached in and pulled out the second item in the box. A onesie. It read, "My dad's pull-out game is weak." Again I chuckled. And again, more tears.

The box fell off my leg and hit the ground while I held the small piece of fabric in my hand. I rubbed it softly with my thumb, thinking of my wife, the pain she was in, and the fact that there wasn't a single thing I could do to make it better.

"Holy shit," I heard someone exclaim. "Call an ambulance!"

I was on the floor again. This time in the bathroom. I think I was still in the bathroom. The music wasn't as loud wherever I was. But it was hot—my skin was boiling. My chest hurt more than it ever had, and my heart sounded like it was trying to break free of my chest.

Could I blame it? I wanted out too.

"Just breathe."

Hearing Natalie's voice didn't help the pain I was in.

"I think he's having a heart attack," someone said.

But I couldn't see anyone. Even with my eyes open, everything was blurry.

Maybe they were right. Maybe it was a heart attack. Maybe I was dying. Would that really be so bad? Did I really care if I didn't survive?

***

My eyes fluttered open, seeing Mark next to me, and a curtain hanging in the air just on the other side of him.

"Jesus Christ," he said, putting his hand to his chest. "Your mom would have fucking killed me if I had let you die."

I wished he had. But saying that wouldn't help.

"What happened?" I asked, but while my memory was hazy, I remembered more than I cared to. I was more interested in what he had seen.

The curtain moved and who I presumed to be my doctor walked over to me.

"Leo Algar?" he asked.

I nodded.

"I'm Dr. Rodriguez."

"Was it a heart attack?" Mark asked anxiously. "He's only thirty-two. It couldn't be that, right?"

"It wasn't a heart attack," Dr. Rodriguez said with a smile. "Although I'm sure it felt like one."

"What was it then?" Mark asked.

Dr. Rodriguez looked at me to ensure I was listening. Or maybe understanding. "It was a panic attack."

"Oh, shit, that's it?" Mark asked, breathing a sigh of relief.

Dr. Rodriguez looked annoyed but kept his attention on me. "Panic attacks can be pretty scary. Have you had them before?"

"No," I replied. "At least I don't think so."

He nodded.

"What about the bloody nose?" Mark asked.

"Your blood pressure was pretty high when you came in, Mr. Algar. Have you been under a lot of stress lately?"

Dead wife. No job. No kids. No will to live. Stress? Check.

"A little," I replied.

Mark shot me a look.

Dr. Rodriguez noticed.

"Well, I suggest you look into some ways of coping with your stress before you trigger an actual heart attack at some point. Thirty-two or not, people send themselves to an early grave not getting their stress levels in check."

I nodded. But an early grave didn't scare me.

"We have a few more tests we'd like to run, but we should have you out in the next few hours."

I nodded again.

"Thanks, Doc," Mark said as Dr. Rodriguez left the small-secluded area.

"I'm going to go update Beth. I'll be back in a sec."

Before I could respond, he too disappeared behind the curtain.

I rested my head back on the pillow and stared up at the tile. I did what I did at home and found something to count repeatedly until I would hopefully drift off to sleep. Even if it was only for a few minutes.

"Alright, everyone get together with their partner," the dance instructor began. "Hands together, shoulders back—perfect, Leslie. Yes, good. Good job, everyone. Now to the music."

"I thought we were supposed to be learning the tango," I whispered to Natalie. "Not four different steps on repeat."

"All in good time, Mr. Algar," the dance instructor replied from inches behind me.

Natalie giggled. "I thought you hated dancing."

"I mean, I don't love it. But I love you."

"I wish we would have learned it for our wedding," she continued as we danced the few steps we had been shown on repeat.

"If I could go back—" I began.

"—I wouldn't change a thing," she interjected, and then smiled. "I'm just glad we're doing it now."

I swallowed a lump. There was so much I wanted to do with her. So much to see. So much to experience. And time was no longer on our side. I should have done more.

"Hey," she whispered, bringing my eyes to her. "Don't do that."

"Do what?" I replied with a chuckle.

"Don't go away like that. I don't want you blaming yourself."

"I'm not."

"You are."

I looked down at the floor, feeling the tears pooling in the corner of my eyes.

I needed to stop. No tears. No sadness. I had plenty of time for that once she was gone. She was here. She was with me. There would be no tears while she was in my arms. Only laughter.

I looked back up at her and put my arm up and spun her around.

"Somebody's skipping ahead," the instructor teased as Natalie's laughter filled the air, sounding sweeter to me than any melody ever could.

Chapter Seven
{Friday, March 2ⁿᵈ, 2018}

Mark told Beth. Beth eventually told my mom. My mom immediately called me.

She was hysterical.

Why did I become friends with them again?

"It was just a panic attack," I said for the third time to her on the phone.

"You were in the hospital, Leo. That's not anything to be so cavalier about," my mom retorted.

"I was there because they wanted to make sure I was okay, which I was."

"A panic attack doesn't sound okay to me."

"I drank too much."

"That doesn't sound okay to me either."

"Yeah, that wasn't helpful."

I rolled my eyes at Natalie's comment. "Mom, seriously, I'm fine."

She sighed on the other end of the phone. She was going to concede.

"I think I should come stay with you."

"No," I replied, probably quicker than I should have. "I mean, you have Dad and work and Grant."

"Well, then Grant can come stay with—"

Silence. Grant must have been listening—and more than likely shaking his head. We hadn't left things on the best of terms after my visit home at Christmas.

"It's fine, Mom. *I'm* fine."

"I don't like that you two aren't talking."

"We're not talking. We're just busy."

I sensed an eye roll.

Would she believe I was busy? She didn't know I had been put on leave, but I could almost guarantee Grant didn't have a new job. So the busy excuse would only work at most for one.

She sighed. It was the last one before she would fully concede with her thoughts on my well-being. At least for the night.

"Well, then I want weekly calls," she demanded.

"Mom—"

"Oh, I'm sorry. Is that asking too much for the person who gave birth to you, raised you, clothed you, fed you—"

"—Okay, enough with the guilt trip. I'll call you weekly."

"Good. You should've been doing it anyway."

A smile flashed across my face, but only briefly.

"Alright, well, dinner's almost done," she said. "Call me soon and update me."

"On what?" I asked.

"On *you*."

"I don't know if there will be much to update you on."

"That's fine. That means you're staying out of trouble."

I shook my head. "Okay, I'll call you soon. I love you."

"Love you too. Buh-bye."

"Bye," I replied, hanging up the phone.

I set my phone down on the counter, the home screen photo of Natalie and me appearing on the screen.

My arms were around her. Her hair was cut off at the shoulders. Her beautiful green eyes glistened in the sun. She was breathtaking.

I stared at her like I had many times before. But as my eyes gazed into hers, the passing of time registered as the minute clicked to the next on the screen.

"Oh, fuck," I said audibly to myself as I jumped up and went to slip into something that made it look like I knew how to operate a washing machine.

Mark and Beth were having a housewarming party. I was in no shape to go as I hadn't been fully sober in what seemed like months. I looked like I didn't know what a hairbrush or shaver was, and my people skills hadn't seemed to recover since Natalie's departure.

But Mark had been trying. He was checking in on me. He was diving back into our friendship right where we had left off. And although I was having a hard time focusing on any kind of positive at the moment, he himself was an odd glow of light I was trying to hold on to. I needed it so I could stay away from the permanent darkness I had been swirling into.

A knock at the door pulled me from my thoughts.

"Diane," I said as I opened it.

"Good, you're home," she replied as she walked past me into my house.

"Come on in," I said gruffly.

"Don't be like that. Your mom said she's worried about you."

"Jesus, what, do all you women talk?"

"All of us? No. Me and your mother, yes."

"And she talks to Beth."

"Well, *that* I cannot confirm or deny," she replied, glancing around my living room, possibly searching for answers for my mom. "But I told her I would check in."

"Well, I just got off the phone with her."

"The phone can hide things that an in-person visit can't."

"Which is why I like the technology so much," I replied with a deadpan expression. "Speaking of which," I continued. "If you would have used yours, you would know that I am on my way out."

"Oh really? That's convenient."

"No, that's called having a life," I replied. "Regardless of what you and my mom think, I haven't shut myself off from the world."

"Liar."

I rolled my eyes.

"What was that for?" Diane asked, giving me the side-eye.

"Sorry."

That didn't help.

"Well, if you do have plans, where are you going?"

"Housewarming party."

"By yourself?"

"That was the plan."

"So, you wouldn't mind a tag-along."

I chuckled. It took us both by surprise.

"Suit yourself," I replied, my expression shifting back to its cold demeanor.

She raised a brow but stood firm.

"You're driving," I added.

Although it wasn't the best idea to take her to Mark and Beth's, especially unbeknownst to either side, I was delighted to have a designated driver so I could consume more alcohol and keep my buzz.

She pulled her keys out of her jacket and handed me her phone.

"Type in the address and let's go," she said, as if to say, "game on."

Poor woman had no idea what she was walking into.

I shrugged, more to myself, and followed her out the door.

When we got into her car, she put her phone in the holder and clicked out of the GPS briefly, revealing a home screen photo of her own.

It was Natalie and her two years before. They were dressed in purple at one of the Lupus walks they did multiple times a year. I did my best to make it to them all but wasn't always able. Diane, however, never missed a single one.

"I'm sorry. I'm just too tired," Natalie replied to me, her head resting on my lap.

I continued to stroke her hair as her eyelids drooped.

"It's okay. We can always go see a movie tomorrow after school."

"Yeah," she replied. "I'm sorry I've been so out of it lately."

She didn't need to apologize; I was just worried.

"Mom said it's just stress," she continued. "I told her about my body hurting sometimes, but she said that's probably just because I'm tired."

My brows furrowed. "Why don't you have her take you to the doctors anyway? Just to be sure."

She attempted a shrug. Or maybe she was just getting comfortable.

"When Edwin dropped me as his kid, I lost his health insurance."

The mention of her dad made my body tense. I hated him. I hated a person I had never even met. I had known Natalie for seven months and I couldn't imagine ever leaving her. How was it possible her own flesh and blood felt differently after sixteen years?

"You don't have any health insurance at all?" I asked.

"I think we have something through the state, but tests are expensive. And I doubt they'll run them on me anyway. I'm young. I'm stressed. I'm just tired."

I sighed and continued to run my hand through her hair. "Okay, well, then you should sleep."

"No, I don't want you to leave," she replied, her eyes completely shut and not reopening.

I smiled, leaning down and kissing her head. "I'm not going anywhere. Just take a nap."

"You good?" Diane asked.

I glanced over at her, giving her question a second to register, and then I nodded.

"Where'd you go just now?"

"Where I've been going for months," I replied with a shrug. "Back with her."

That was all I needed to say. Diane understood. She was one of the only people on earth who understood what the absence of Natalie really meant for the world we lived in.

"So, who got a new house?" she asked.

We were close enough that I hoped she wouldn't turn back now, or even abandon me on the side of the road.

"Mark and Beth."

Her foot tapped the brake.

Honestly, she probably hadn't intended to do that. It was a reflex. She shot me a look at the same time. "God, you're an asshole." I couldn't tell if she was kidding or not.

More than likely, she wasn't.

***

"Well, I see they haven't changed at all," Diane said as we strolled along the beautiful lit path to the house. "It's a fucking mansion."

"He likes his houses big," I replied.

"He's overcompensating."

"Are you confirming that you've seen him naked?"

"Jesus, I would never imply that."

"You just did."

"You're here!" Mark exclaimed, seeing me as the door opened.

His eyes went swiftly to Diane.

"And you brought… Diane—" he said, his expression fooling no one. "Glad you could make it," he lied.

We walked into the house. There were people everywhere.

"Nice place," I said, looking around.

"Oh, this is nothing. Wait 'til you see the master suite."

Diane exhaled. Did I miss her eye roll?

Mark's expression shifted slightly at her, so I put my hand on his shoulder so his attention was back on me. "I'd love to see it."

"I'm going to get a drink," Diane said.

She took off in one direction as he led me in another.

"So, is there a reason you felt like torturing us all tonight?" he asked when we were alone in the hallway.

I shook my head. "Well, if your wife wouldn't tell my mom shit she doesn't need to know, then Diane wouldn't be checking up on me out of the blue."

He sighed. "Noted. But she was just worried."

"Yeah, I know. Doesn't make it any less annoying."

"The master suite!" he exclaimed as he pushed open the French doors and moved past my comment.

I peered around the room. The high ceilings made the room look bigger than it was. A large bay window opened up to the beautifully landscaped, private, and well-lit backyard.

"Yeah, I figured you'd like that the best," he said, slapping my shoulder. "You should see it in the daylight. It's no Leo Algar design, but they didn't do half bad."

I smiled.

"Mark?" I heard Beth ask right before she appeared in the doorway. "Did you see Diane is—oh, Leo, I didn't know you had arrived."

"Does that explain *Diane*?" I asked.

She furrowed her brow. "It does. Not that I mind. I just didn't remember inviting her."

"Yeah, she's my plus one."

"Well, remind me to deny you plus ones in the future," Mark said.

My brows furrowed. "What do you have against her?"

"Nothing," he replied, his expression shifting. "I'm just giving you shit."

"No, I mean, you've always disliked her. Why?"

He looked caught off guard. I would've been too. It was out of left field. I never cared before.

"How about we get you two some drinks?" Beth said.

I wasn't sure how booze was going to help with that exact situation, but I knew it would help the rest of them.

"I don't know what to do anymore, man," I said to Mark as I polished off the fifth I had paid the bartender to leave in front of me.

"It can't be that bad."

I exhaled, sliding the glass off to the side. "Not that bad? Nat hates me."

"She doesn't hate you," he replied with a laugh. "That woman thinks you walk on water."

I shook my head but didn't respond.

It had been a little over two years since she had miscarried on Valentine's Day. Since then, it had happened two more times. Mark and Diane knew about the first. The other two we kept to ourselves.

After the third one, Natalie went to the doctor. After months of tests, she found out she had lupus. Many things made sense after that. But many things also fell apart. Including us.

Instead of a focus on family, she concentrated solely on work. It seemed to make her happy, so I did the same with mine. But a month of that turned into a few months. And a few months turned into a year. Now we barely spoke. We were busy. We were ships passing in the night. We were distant. We were burned out. We were broken.

"We haven't had sex in three months," I said.

His head turned so fast I thought it was going to keep spinning into a 360.

"No way."

I nodded and lifted the glass I had emptied. I had a feeling the bartender had cut me off.

"I think she's going to leave me."

Mark's expression was somber. He was the voice of reasoning when I was unreasonable. He was my positivity when I had lost it all.

So, where were those words? Where was the reasoning? Where was the positivity?

"She's going to leave me, isn't she?" I asked, tears welling up in my eyes.

He finished his drink like he knew something I didn't.

"Do you and Beth know something? Did she say something?" I asked the questions in quick succession as I moved my body towards his.

What wasn't he wasn't telling me?

"Did she meet someone? Is there someone else?"

His brows furrowed. "Come on, you know that woman only has eyes for you."

I shook my head. "I don't know what I know anymore," I replied, backing away from him. "We've never not talked about everything. I've never been in the dark about what she's feeling."

"Maybe she's just going through something," he said.

It was an attempt at positivity though it needed some work.

"But why can't I go through it with *her? Why can't she lean on me?"*

"Maybe it's something you can't help her with."

"Yeah, maybe. Or maybe she's just trying to find an easy way to leave me."

I looked to Mark for some reassurance that I was wrong in everything I was saying. And unfortunately for my less than sober self, he didn't have any to give.

"Chug, chug, chug—"

I glanced up from my drink that I was certain Mark had handed me at some point and saw Diane doing a beer bong.

I glanced around, disoriented for a second. Was this a memory or present day—post Natalie?

The tube left Diane's mouth as she wiped her lips and threw her hands in the air. "Fuck, yeah, still got it," she shouted.

I smirked and took a sip of whatever was in my glass.

Diane wiped at some beer that had made its way onto her silk blouse. I was certain she hadn't expected to end up with beer on it when she picked it out that morning.

"Someone's loosening up," Mark said as he nudged my side.

He seemed a little proud, like his party had made that happen.

And maybe it had, but Diane was more fun than she seemed. She was reserved and quiet to most. But she wasn't as prudish or cold as Mark seemed to think she was. He had just never taken the time to get to know her.

"I thought this was a housewarming party—for adults," I joked. "Where'd the beer bong come from?"

"He probably has them planted throughout the house," Beth replied as she stepped next to me.

"Nah, I just found it when I was unpacking. Ethan's the one who got it out."

"Ethan's here?"

Mark nodded as he took a drink.

I hadn't seen Ethan since the funeral. Before that, I hadn't seen him since Natalie had gotten sick. He had taken over as my pseudo-best friend when Mark vanished from my life. I felt like a shitty person for using him as a replacement, and then vanishing on him when Natalie found out about Glenn—her cancer.

However, he didn't seem to hold it against me. But maybe it was because it was hard to be mad at me. I was a shell of the person I used to be. Maybe he was glad he got out when he did. I was surprised Mark wasn't. Maybe that was just what best friends did?

But then again, why leave in the first place?

"Why did you stop talking to me?" I asked, looking at Mark.

Diane glanced over at me from across the room as if she had heard my question. But with her distance, and the music, I knew she couldn't have.

My eyes left hers and wandered back over to Mark who had yet to respond.

"Why can't we just leave the past in the past?" he asked, annoyed, then walked away.

That was unusual for him. Even at my worst, he never got annoyed or angry. He took my moods in stride and let them roll off his back. It used to make me kind of resentful, how he could be such a great friend to me. He was flawed. I could see that. But he never was with me. So, it made me question his vanishing act even more.

"—It's my life, it's now or never—" I sang as my arm hung around Mark's neck while he helped me to my door.

"—Okay Bon Jovi, I think you might want to quiet it down before your wife kills us both for waking her."

"No, she won't kill me—" I began as we reached the front door. "—She's just going to divorce me."

The door opened as the words left my mouth. I don't know what was heard.

124

"Natalie!" Mark exclaimed, plastering a smile on his face.

She didn't do the same.

"By the way you're carrying him, I'm assuming he's drunk."

"Your assumption would be right," he said.

"Well, can you at least get him up the stairs into the bed?" she asked.

I hate that she wasn't speaking directly to me. That said it all, right?

Mark helped me past her as she shut the door.

"Well, she's up if you want to keep singing," Mark whispered to me.

I think he just wanted to dull the uncomfortable silence between my wife and me.

I did too.

But singing wasn't going to do the trick any longer.

"I got it," I said when we reached the stairs.

I shifted away from him and immediately crashed into the wall.

"Mark, can you please help him up the stairs?" Natalie asked.

She didn't sound annoyed. Which would've made sense. Instead, she sounded sad.

I hated that I made her sad. I wished I made her anything else other than that.

"I got it," I said again, standing myself up from the wall.

"Yup, I know," Mark said. "I'm just going to walk with you."

He was following Natalie's directions. She didn't want me to fall down the stairs. That was nice of her at least.

Mark followed me up the stairs as I clutched the railing, trying not to make anyone's night worse with me splitting my head on the tile at the bottom.

Shortly after, Natalie followed behind.

I was surprised she hadn't told him to dump me on the couch. Or leave me outside.

Why was I surprised? She wasn't bitter or vindictive. She was sad.

She was also angry. But was it at me? I really didn't know anymore.

"Thanks for bringing him home," she told him.

"Of course," he replied as I walked into the bedroom, kicked off my shoes, and fell into bed.

"How much did he drink?" she asked as they stood by the bedroom doorway.

I wrapped my arms around my pillow, holding the only thing I had been able to in my bed for months.

"A fifth of Jack."

She didn't respond.

"I'm surprised he was as lucid as he was," he said.

"Yeah, well, he's built up a tolerance lately."

The air was silent again.

"Walk me out?" Mark asked.

"Sure," she replied as I heard them walk away.

The room spun, even with my eyes shut. But I didn't want to sleep. Not until she was beside me.

I wanted to make sure she was coming to bed. I wanted to make sure that, if this was our last night together, we at least spent it sharing the same space.

Time was as fluid as the contents of the bottle I had consumed. I had no idea at what rate it was passing. It didn't help my nerves that were supposed to be numb.

But as the door creaked and then closed, I felt the tension in my body subside ever so slightly.

The light was still on as I opened my eyes enough to see her walk to the closet. She glanced in the full-length mirror, an expression crossing her face I had never seen before. I didn't know what to make of it.

She rubbed the sleeve of her baggy sweatshirt that hung over her pajama shorts, looking deep in thought.

Where was she? What was she thinking? Was her head in the same place mine was? Was this our last night? Was she ready to run in the morning?

"I love you," I said, though I wasn't sure how clearly my words had been received.

She turned to face me. "What?"

"I love you," I repeated.

Her expression shifted. It was softer. Sadder.

Why did I make her so sad?

She crawled into bed and leaned her back up against the headboard.

She looked like she was going to speak, but I was nervous to hear what she had to say, so I started talking instead.

"I'm sorry I'm a bad husband. I wanted to be better for you. I wanted to give you everything you've ever dreamed of—" I said as I did my best to shift myself up. But the room spun some more. "I failed you."

"You failed me?" she asked, her eyes meeting mine. I wasn't sure when she had started crying, but a few tears fell silently as she wiped them away. "You didn't fail me, Leo. I failed me," she replied. "I failed us."

Confusion fell over me while I pushed through the spinning and brought my body to sit beside her. "How in the world could you possibly think you failed yourself? Or us?"

Her brows furrowed. "I can't give you the life I promised."

"What are you talking about?" I asked, reaching for her hand.

She pulled away, her eyes falling to the floor. "The lupus, Leo. You didn't plan for that."

"I mean, I did, in sickness and in health was a big part of the vows," I said with a smirk.

She didn't laugh. "Is that why you're still here?" she asked. "Out of obligation?"

My eyes widened. The shift in my body made me feel nauseous. "What?"

"Are you still here—with me—because of our vows?"

I grabbed for her hand, and that time she let me take it. "I would be here regardless of what we said that day. Regardless of any fucking piece of paper."

"But why?"

"What do you mean?"

"I'm sick, Leo. This isn't what you signed up for. The unbelievable headaches and muscle pain, the nausea, the anxiety, the depression, the—" Her eyes welled up with tears and spilled over. "—I can't give you the family you deserve."

I threw my arms around her, pulling her to my chest. I was certain it was more ungraceful than it felt to me.

"Babe, I promise you, you're the only family I need."

"Leo," I heard just before I felt someone grab my arm and shake it.

The memory of the night I had thought my marriage was over stayed fresh in my head. The night that ended up being the one that may have saved it.

"Leo," they said again.

I glanced over at Ethan. "Hey, uh, sorry—" I began, but got distracted as I looked at Mark across the room.

The night that things had started to recover with Natalie was the same time things had dissipated completely with Mark. Had that been the last time I had seen him?

Ethan returned to my side and handed me a napkin, stopping my thoughts. "Your nose is bleeding," he whispered.

"Thanks," I said as I grabbed it from him and pressed it to my face.

"I know it's none of my business how you choose to grieve…"

I raised my brow.

"—But drugs aren't the answer."

My expression stayed intact. What was he talking about?

He moved to stand in front of me. Possibly blocking others from seeing the mess my nose had made, or maybe to prevent them from seeing his scolding of whatever he thought I was up to.

"I've heard you lost your job. You've been moody and spacy—and now, nosebleeds?"

"I didn't lose my job. I'm on leave."

He put up his hand. "Okay, regardless. Again, I'm not judging, I'm just saying, there are other ways to deal with this."

"With what? My wife's death?"

"Yes, that. And everything since."

I rolled my eyes. "I'm sorry, and you would know this how?"

"I've read up on some things."

"Great. Well, you keep reading. We can talk when you've lost the love of your life," I said bitterly. "Now, please excuse me while I tend to my non-drug-related nosebleed."

I held the napkin to my nose and walked to the bathroom, getting a few questionable looks from Mark and Beth's guests.

When I got to the bathroom, the bleeding stopped, and I washed my face.

"You need to control your stress levels."

"That's easier said than done, Nat."

I used the bottom of my shirt to dry off my face, knowing full well it didn't help my disheveled look.

I peered at myself in the mirror. Something I hadn't done in a while. It was strange to know you were inside the body of someone you didn't know. The man looked hollow. He *was* hollow. No, he was angry. Apparently, he was on drugs. Maybe he should be. Maybe that would be a nice change of pace.

There was a knock on the bathroom door.

Didn't I get privacy anymore?

Probably not. That would just give me time to do drugs.

I rolled my eyes before opening the door.

"What?" I asked, before seeing it was Mark, though that may not have changed my question or my tone.

"Ethan was worried about you."

"Ethan thinks I'm high."

"Are you?"

"Can I be?"

"Depends what you brought."

Oh, Mark. Cool as ever. I didn't know him well enough to know what he was into, but the Mark I knew before only smoked weed on occasion and did shrooms a handful of times.

I only indulged in pot occasionally and one time with the shrooms.

He wouldn't judge if I was doing drugs. More than likely he would kick everyone out and ask to do them with me.

My best friend.

I smiled.

Maybe I was on drugs.

"Damn, dude, is Ethan right?"

I shook my head. "Mark, you're my best friend—"

He laughed. "Of course I am. Always will be," he retorted.

My smile fell. "Then why did you leave?"

His expression followed mine. "Leo, I'm not doing this."

He was no longer annoyed. He was angry.

But why?

He turned and began walking away.

I caught up to him, extending my arm so he was blocked between me and the wall.

"Mark, stop. You need to tell me what I did."

He shook his head, keeping his eyes from mine.

"Mark!" I exclaimed.

"Leo," Beth said from behind me.

I didn't move.

"Leo, just stop," she continued.

"No. He was my best friend. What did I do that was so bad?" I asked, the pain resonating in my voice.

"You didn't do anything," Beth said.

"Beth," Mark exclaimed.

"Stop defending her. He deserves to know."

"Know what?" I asked, my arm falling to my side.

"Nothing," Mark said, taking a step back. "Beth, just stop."

"No. He's not the bad guy here and he shouldn't think he is."

Mark stopped fighting. Beth's shoulders fell just a little and tension settled. Well, at least for her.

"Natalie told Mark she loved him."

My brows furrowed.

Of course she loved him. We all did. It was Mark. He had been our family for years.

Beth read my expression.

"She kissed him, Leo."

"What?" I scoffed.

Her eyes stayed on me. She wasn't changing her words. She wasn't taking them back.

"She said she had been in love with him for quite some time."

"No," I said, shaking my head. "Mark's my best friend."

I looked at him, but he didn't say anything.

"Yeah, which is why he didn't tell you. He didn't want to hurt you."

I shook my head but was having trouble turning my thoughts into words.

"She wouldn't do that," I finally said.

I knew Natalie. She loved me. She had always loved me.

"That was why we left. Mark didn't want to tell you, and I didn't want him around her. I'm sorry, Leo, but she had no right to do that. To either of us. I don't care what was going on in your marriage Mark had one of his own."

"Beth," Mark said.

"She was going to leave you for Mark, but when he turned her down, I guess she decided to stay."

"Stop," I said, catching her off guard. But I wasn't sure why. She had to see what her words were doing to me.

"I'm sorry, Leo, but she wasn't the saint you thought she was."

She said that more sympathetically. But she also seemed to derive some pleasure from it too.

"Leo, I'm sorry," Mark said as I ran my hand through my hair.

What was he sorry for? The fact that my wife loved him? The fact that I was a consolation prize? The fact that she had lied to me for the few years since?

If she lied about him, about us? What else had she lied about?

The pain I had grown accustomed to in my chest was taking over full force, making it hard to breathe. Was I having another panic attack?

A large part of me was hoping it was a heart attack for real that time. God, was I done with the torture the world was bringing me. Not only had it given Natalie to me, it had also taken her away. And then after, when all I had were the memories, it decided to ruin those too.

"Leo!" I heard Mark yell.

I was walking away. Running? Maybe I was running away. I was exiting Mark's house before I had even realized I was moving. But I needed to get away. I needed to make sense of what I had just heard.

I made it to the end of the drive before Diane called after me. "Leo, where you goin'?"

Where *was* I going?

I paused and looked around as I tried to catch my breath. Either I was very out of shape, or the impending panic attack was making it hard to do.

"Leo," Diane said again as she reached me and put her hand on my arm. "You just gonna abandon me with those vultures?" she asked with a chuckle until her eyes met mine. "Hey," she stated softly.

I looked away, and she put her hand to my chin and made me face her.

"Hey," she said, more firmly that time. "What happened?"

"She loved Mark," I replied.

Confusion fell over her face.

"Natalie. Natalie loved Mark—" I continued.

She shook her head. "Leo, what are you talking about?"

"Don't lie for her!" I exclaimed. "She loved him. She kissed him. She was going to leave me. That was why he left—"

"—What are you talking about?"

My heart was pounding in my chest. I was nauseous. I was going to throw up.

"Leo," she said, trying to gain back my attention. "Who told you that?"

"Beth."

She rolled her eyes.

"Consider your sources, Leo."

Now I wore the questionable look.

"Leo, Nat loved you. How could you ever doubt that?"

"I didn't—she's not here, how am I supposed to ask her—"

"You shouldn't have to," she said bitterly. "You know her better than that."

"I thought I did—"

Her hand hit my cheek. It stung, but the act of having it done hurt more.

"Don't you for one fucking second doubt how that woman felt about you!" she yelled, her pointer finger pushing into my chest. "She was an amazing wife—an amazing human."

"I know that—but then why would they say that?"

"Because *Mark* loved *her*!" she exclaimed.

"What?"

"Leo, we need to go," she said, starting to walk to the car.

I grabbed her hand, stopping her in her tracks.

"You don't get to say that and then act like you didn't."

"We can talk, just not here."

"No, fuck that. I want to know now!"

She looked frustrated with me, but even more so, herself.

"Mark knew you guys were having issues and he kissed her."

"When?"

"I don't know. One of the nights he brought you home drunk."

My brows furrowed.

"He helped you to your room, Natalie walked him to the door, and he told her he loved her."

"He wouldn't do that."

"Oh, but your wife would?" she retorted in disgust.

"No, neither of them would do this. None of this makes sense."

"Leo, he's been in love with her since college."

My eyes met hers. "What are you talking about?" I asked, shaking my head. "You're just saying that because you hate him."

"I didn't always hate him."

"Yes, you did."

"No, when we all first started hanging out, before Beth, I had a crush on him. He was loud and stupid, but for some reason I was attracted to that."

She seemed disgusted with herself.

"I started paying more attention to him. The way he talked to her, the way he looked at her. It was the same way you did."

I shook my head. "He loved her because we were family."

"He idolized you, Leo. He always has. He wanted what you had. That included her."

My face was wet. I wished it was tears. But it wasn't. Goddamn bloody nose.

"Calm down. Breathe."

"Calm down?" I yelled, taking Diane by surprise. I ran my hands aggressively through my hair.

"Leo, you're bleeding."

"I know," I said, wiping at my face and turning towards the house.

"Where are you going?"

"To see my *best* friend."

I barreled through the front door and made a beeline for Mark.

He looked scared. As he should have. He knew he was lying, and now I knew it too.

"Leo," he began, putting his hands up in front of him.

The person he had been talking to stepped aside, and I pushed Mark against the wall.

"Leo!" I heard Beth exclaim as I put my hand around Mark's neck.

"You fucking kissed her!" I yelled, my voice sounding foreign to my ears.

"Leo—" he tried to say.

"—Don't fucking lie to me, Mark!"

His eyes were full of terror. But was it because of my anger or the truth?

"Leo, stop!" Diane said as I felt her hands on my arm, trying to pull it off his neck.

Out of all the people there, I was surprised she was the one trying to stop me.

"He tried to steal my wife!"

"But he didn't!" she said.

"You were my best friend!" I yelled directly in his face, the words seizing my chest. "You were my best friend and I lost *you* because you loved *her*."

"I'm sorry," he whispered, either so Beth wouldn't hear, or because I was cutting off his oxygen supply.

"I don't fucking care what you are. You're dead to me," I said, releasing my grip. "But unlike with my wife, I won't be grieving you."

I turned around and exited the house as quickly as I had entered. Diane followed closely behind, and Mark's apologies echoed to me until the car door slammed shut.

"What am I going to do after you're gone?" I asked as we sat on the porch swing.

"What do you mean?" Natalie asked.

"I don't have anyone else."

"You have Diane."

"No, you have Diane," I replied with a smile.

"Well, I'm not taking her with me. So, you'll have her. Plus you got Ethan, and your parents, and Grant."

"I wish Mark was still around."

She was quiet. She hadn't said much about Mark disengaging from our lives a few years before.

She seemed indifferent to his absence. But she didn't get it. If Diane left, she would understand. But she still had her best friend.

Maybe Diane and I would have more to talk about when Natalie was gone.

The thought sent an ache through my chest.

"I should have been a better friend," I said.

She shifted her head up from my chest and looked at me, stopping the swing with her feet on the ground. "Leo, you're an amazing friend. You did nothing to make him leave."

"No, I could have been better—"

"—What is it you always say to me about Edwin?"

Shit, she was bringing up her dad. She wasn't playing around.

"That he's a piece of shit," I replied.

She laughed. "Besides that."

"That him leaving was about him and not about you."

"Right. So can't that same logic be applied to Mark?"

"It just doesn't make sense."

"Babe, things don't always make sense. You guys had an amazing friendship. Just remember it for what it was. That's what helps me with Edw—my dad. I had years of memories made with him. I love those memories. But that man is gone, even if he's still alive. The man who raised me died the moment he chose a new family over me. I've come to terms with that. And I think you will too. Mark is your past, baby. It's time to move on."

Chapter Eight

{Saturday, April 7ᵗʰ, 2018}

"This message is a reminder for Leo Algar that you have an appointment with Dr. Grayling on Friday April 20th at 2:30pm. If you cannot make this appointment, please call the office first thing Monday morning. Thank you."

I locked my phone and set it on the counter as I went back to cleaning out the hallway closet. I had already gone through the rest of the closets in the house, except for the one in the bedroom.

I considered Natalie and me to be pretty clean and organized adults, much better than when we were teens. But closets—and the fact they had a door to close on them—were our downfall. They were vertical junk drawers in our home. A catch-all of everything we just couldn't let go of.

Maybe that was why I was purging them now. Not because I was ready to move on, but because I needed more room to store the things I couldn't part with.

Could I bottle up my memories of Natalie and put them in the closet?

I slid a tote out from the bottom of the pile and kneeled next to it on the floor. Each closet came with its own set of reminders of the life I had lost. It was cruel. But I was only doing it to myself.

Since Mark's party and losing the one person I thought could pull me out of the darkness, I felt like I had gone mad. My caring had been low, and my anger had been high, but they both found new depths inside of me I didn't know were possible. It was how I started cleaning. The memories of Natalie calmed me, creating a little escape of her presence.

It would bring my blood pressure down to normal ranges. I only knew that because I had been wearing a blood pressure watch for the past week.

After Mark's party and my third bloody nose, Diane made me go to the doctor. She told me to make the appointment, or she was going to tell my mom. Sometimes I really hated people.

I had been calling my mom like I said I would. Beth had either stopped talking to her after I had outed her husband's love for my wife in front of her and their guests, or my mom wasn't bringing it up. Most likely the former.

Mark had been calling at least once a week and leaving an apology message. I hoped they would stop soon. I should have listened to Natalie and just moved on. I could have lived a lifetime never knowing what I had found out. I hated what he did. I hated that what he did made her keep something from me. We didn't have secrets. Or I thought so anyway.

My watch beeped.

"Breathe. Don't get yourself so worked up."

My watch beeped a few more times and then stopped.

I opened the tote, discovering an old laptop of mine on top. It was heavy and hadn't worked in years. It was the first one I owned and, after six years of faithful service, it just stopped working. Everything on it was lost.

I plugged Natalie's Sony digital camera into one end of the cord and then plugged the other into the laptop.

"I can't believe your mom got you a computer," she said.

I shrugged. "She was told it will come in handy for college next year."

Natalie nodded and then shifted to sit on my lap. I loved when she did that.

I maneuvered my arms around her to the computer as I clicked what I needed to in order to upload the pictures.

One by one they started to cross the screen.

"Jesus, woman, how many photos did you take?"

"As many as the camera would hold. That's why I needed them on here, so I could take more."

I shook my head and smiled. "Wait a second," I said. "Was that a picture of me sleeping?"

She giggled. "You looked so peaceful."

"You're creepy," I replied as I poked her side.

"Well, don't look so damn good and I won't want to take pictures of you."

"Noted."

I wrapped my arms around her midsection as the rest of the photos uploaded.

"I'm going to have to get a new computer if you keep taking photos at this speed."

"No, just get a disk or zip drive to save it on."

"Zip drive?"

"It's a device that holds information or pictures and such on it instead of it having to stay on the computer."

I raised my brow.

"I've never used one. My da—Edwin had one for his computer."

I nodded, needing no further explanation that made her talk about him.

"I'm good with them being on my computer. And when this gets full, we'll get another one."

"Computers aren't cheap, my man. You planning on making your parents buy you another one?"

I laughed. "No, I'll get a job to pay for it."

Natalie adjusted her body so she was straddling me.

"No job," she said. "I want to spend every second I can with you."

"You know we'll have to work eventually, right?" I asked with a laugh. "I want a place of our own."

There was a knock at my bedroom door that was opened a few inches.

"Dinner," my mom said.

I was glad she didn't walk in and see Natalie on my lap. The last thing I needed was another sex talk from my dad.

"Okay," I said, as Natalie smirked.

"I want a place of our own too," she said, kissing the tip of my nose. "But...no jobs until after high school. Let's just be kids with no responsibilities for one more year."

I grabbed the laptop and cord out of the tote and walked with it to the kitchen. I pulled out my phone and looked up computer repair places.

The one I wanted was a few towns over and open until 7:00.

I was certain the computer was a lost cause. But maybe it still had some worth.

***

A bell rang above the door as I opened it. The noise was jarring. Maybe because I hadn't been out of the house in days. Maybe because the space I had stepped into was dingy and overcrowded with broken technology of the past.

I looked back at the door.

It seemed I had taken a time machine into the nineties. For a moment that thought was comforting. At least Natalie was alive then.

"Can I help you?" I heard.

My wrist beeped.

I took a deep breath and turned around.

"Uh, yeah, hi. Do you fix computers?" I asked, then shook my head. "I mean, obviously that's what you do. I, uh, have a computer I need fixed."

He looked me up and down and raised his eyebrows. I may have looked as disheveled and unorganized as my junk drawer closets, but at least I was still showering regularly. That had to be something, right?

"Okay," he finally responded. Maybe he wasn't used to the outside world either. His appearance was in similar shambles. "Let's see what you got."

He stood a few inches shorter than me and weighed a buck eighty at most. His glasses made him look smarter, or maybe he actually needed them to read.

I handed the computer over to him.

"Fujitsu PC I-4187?" he asked. But he was speaking a foreign language to me.

"Sure."

He smiled. "I haven't seen one in years. Most people gave up on these when all the newer upgrades came out. When did it stop working?"

"Eight years ago? Maybe nine?"

"And you're just now trying to repair it?" he asked, not looking up as he opened it and sized it up.

"My wife had it packed up and I just found it."

He nodded. "Okay, well, I'll see what I can do. But no promises."

I nodded in response, but he didn't see it. "Should I leave my number?"

"Sure thing. Let me grab you a piece of paper and pen," he said, getting up and disappearing into the back. "Here you go."

I took them from him, wrote down my info and handed it over.

"Thanks, Leo," he said, reading the paper. "I should know more sometime this week."

"Perfect," I replied, forcing a smile.

146

"Name's Ned by the way. Sorry, manners have been lost on me lately."

I nodded.

Me too.

I set down the pen, seeing a picture of Ned and a little girl.

"You got kids?" I asked unexpectedly.

"Sure do. Two of them."

"Oh yeah?" I asked, glancing over at him.

He smiled fondly. "Yeah, Emma Jean and Benny—well, Ben. He says he's too old for Benny now."

His smile faded.

I didn't respond. Possibly making it weird.

"Well, thanks for the help," I said, pulling him from his slightly dazed appearance.

"Sure thing."

***

When I got back home, I went through the rest of the tote and finished up deciding what to keep and what to get rid of. My living room was a shrine to my past life. I shouldn't have chosen the room I had been sleeping in to put it all in. It wasn't going to be as easy to ignore or turn away like I had done months before with my wedding photo.

Around six in the evening, I had already finished a fifth of Jack and opened a new one. It was the only thing that dulled the sting of each room. God, I hated it there.

"You don't hate our house."

"No, but I hate it without you," I replied, taking another swig straight from the bottle.

"And this is the master bedroom," the realtor, Kathy, said, walking to the middle of the room, and holding her hands out as if to say, wow.

But she didn't have to. Natalie said it instead.

"So you like it?" I asked with a smile.

"Don't you?" she replied, her eyes wide as she walked to the window overlooking the backyard.

"We can walk out there next," Kathy added, then looked at me. "I hear that's your concern."

"My only concern is what that woman likes," I replied, nodding my head towards Natalie who looked nothing shy of giddy at the potential of that being our new home.

"I want you to like it too," Natalie replied, walking back over to me.

"I love it. But I also loved the last ten houses we saw."

I knew she thought I was just saying that, but I really did. I didn't care where we lived. My promotion was taking us away from our home. Away from her mom, away from my parents, away from our friends.

She was so supportive. So didn't hesitate to tell me to take it, knowing what that meant for her life, and her job.

I'm sure it helped that Diane was relocating too. But that didn't come until after Natalie had agreed to the move.

So I wanted her to pick. I wanted her to decide where we would be spending our nights.

"I love it," Natalie said.

"Yeah?" Kathy beamed.

"Yeah, I can see a future here."

"But you couldn't in the last ten?" I teased.

She playfully slapped my arm. "I don't know what it is," she began. "I just knew it from the moment we walked in. This is our home."

The excitement on Natalie's face was fresh in my mind even though that day was a few years after we were married.

The pure joy in her eyes warmed my heart at that time. She had such hope for our future. A future of kids to fill the rooms. A future of hosting parties in the backyard. A future of growing old together in the house we had first picked out, because it was perfect and nothing else would compare.

But she was hopeful for a future she didn't get.

I was stuck in a house that reminded me of that.

And with the memory fading, the rage I had been trying to contain rushed to the surface as I grabbed my keys off the counter and slammed the front door behind me.

***

The hum of the engine was barely audible against the beeping of my wrist. It was constant. And it was fucking annoying.

The doctor would want to know what caused my high blood pressure.

My wife's death, I would reply bitterly.

He would then ask, what caused it that day? At that particular time?

I would respond that Jack was the culprit.

He suspected my drinking was a factor. He could smell it on my breath when I was there. I was all but brushing my teeth with it now.

I had once thought doctors' offices were terrifying. But I wasn't scared to get bad news anymore. When you've lived through the worst, nothing more could hurt you.

I was invincible.

The door to the repair shop opened and shut. I watched from my car as Ned locked up and began his walk to his car.

He drove a silver Buick LeSabre. That was my guess anyway as it was the only one left in the lot besides mine.

I opened my car door as he approached his Buick.

"Hey," I said, causing him to turn around.

"Leo," he replied. "I started working on the computer this afternoon—" he continued as I approached him.

The closer I got, the more his demeanor shifted.

It was possible the beeping on my wrist was throwing him off, adding a little tension to the air. Or maybe it was the expression I held which looked far from casual chitchat about the state of my computer.

"Are you okay?" he asked when I got within feet of him.

But my reply was my fist to his face.

No, I'm not okay.

But the words didn't come out.

"What the hell!" he yelled, grabbing his nose just before it started to bleed.

He took a minute to retaliate. But when he did, he sent the body weight he did have back into me.

But the landing of his punch didn't pack as much as mine did. Not because of the weight difference. More so because I had caught him off guard. He had to go from casual conversation about a computer to a disgruntled customer—and fast.

Unfortunately for him, I wasn't giving him time to catch up.

I hit him again and then shoved him into the side of his car.

"I don't understand," he said, beginning to cower at my fists.

Landing another hit to his face, blood seemed to pour from his mouth. He had either bitten his tongue or lost a tooth.

The beeping of my wrist rang through my ears, causing me to take note of the faucet of blood that was flowing from my nose as well.

It was possible that my rapidly beating heart was pumping it out faster than normal.

In my brief distraction, Ned attempted to run. But I grabbed the back of his shirt and tugged it—his body crashed against the ground.

"Who are you? What do you want?" he pleaded.

"I don't want anything from you, *Ned*," I said sharply.

"Then why are you doing this?"

I pulled back my foot and sent it into his stomach. Then I did it two more times before I heard a scream. But it wasn't his. For a moment I thought it was Natalie's.

I glanced behind me to see a woman on the sidewalk looking horrified.

She made eye contact with me, her phone to her ear. I wanted to tell her it was okay. That I wouldn't hurt her. But I was covered in blood. Both his and mine. I was beeping as if I had my own personal alarm to sound for people to run from me.

I took a step towards her and she ran. Then within seconds, sirens filled the airwaves.

I glanced at Ned's body on the ground.

He wasn't dead. But he was playing dead. I was sure a coward like that had the instinct to just lie there.

"You have *three* kids, *Edwin*. Learn how to fucking count."

The shouting from the police echoed through my head as the beeping continued. But as they reached me, the already dark and gloomy world faded the rest of the way. Blacking out everything that had been left of the life I had without her.

"So, I was thinking," Natalie began as she placed her coffee down on the table and then her body on my lap.

"Well, that's always terrifying."

She playfully pushed at my shoulder. "Shut up," she retorted. "I was thinking that maybe I should call Edwin."

My brows furrowed. "Why?"

She shrugged but didn't make eye contact with me. "I mean, I know we haven't talked since he left…"

"—Yeah, fifteen years ago."

She nodded. "Yeah, but I mean, shouldn't I give him a chance for closure?"

I was dumbfounded by my wife. She wanted to give that man closure? He didn't deserve to even look at her, let alone get closure from her death.

"Maybe it's a little for me, too," she said, her eyes glossing over.

She rarely talked about him. When she did, it had to do with a random memory from her past, that whether she liked it or not, had him in it.

"If you are doing it for you, then I fully support it. But you don't owe that man anything."

She nodded.

I took my hands and brought her head down to mine, kissing it.

"You tell me what you need, and I'll make it happen."

"Leo," I heard Diane say before I saw her.

My eyelids were heavy, so it took a few moments for me to successfully lift them.

Once I did, I saw I was in a hospital room. It wasn't where I had expected to be. And Diane wasn't who I expected to see.

She looked relieved that I was awake but pissed as hell.

"What the fuck were you thinking?" she asked, but then put up her hand. "Wait, please don't answer that." She took a deep breath. "My intern's at the office now making some calls on my behalf.

They're planning on transferring you to the county jail in the next few hours. I'm hoping to secure your release before that happens."

"Secure my release?" I asked, before looking around, noticing and then feeling the handcuffs holding me to the side of the bed.

"Leo, you beat the shit out of someone. Are you that drunk you don't remember? Wait, don't answer that," she said again. "Did your nosebleed start before or after the fight?"

"During," I replied.

"I see you were wearing your blood pressure watch. When did that start beeping?"

"In the car."

She nodded. "Okay, we can use that."

My brows furrowed. "Use what?"

"You being sick. The high blood pressure—the bloody noses."

I shook my head.

"I'm not sick. I got drunk. I drove to the repair shop. I beat the shit out of him."

"Leo, shut up. As your lawyer, I seriously need you to stop fucking saying shit like that."

"What does it matter? Eat three meals at home; eat three meals behind bars. It all feels like a prison anyway."

Diane's phone buzzed in her hands. She answered it, keeping her eyes from mine.

After a minute, she hit end on her phone and brought her attention back to me.

154

"Alright, so, you didn't leave your keys in the ignition and no one saw you driving the car. So they're not going after a drunk driving charge. But they are looking to charge you with aggravated assault."

I didn't speak. What was there to say?

"Bail is going to be pretty fucking high on this one. What do you have in the bank?"

"Some hefty overdraft fees."

"What do you mean?" she asked as her brows furrowed. "What happened to your 401k's you cashed out last year?"

"Spent. It ran out about three months ago."

"What about Natalie's life insurance?"

"They put the payment on hold while they look into whether it has to be paid out or not."

"What? Since when?"

I shrugged. "I got the letter last month, maybe?"

"Leo, why didn't you tell me?"

"Pretty sure that's not your area of expertise."

"No, but I know people."

"It doesn't matter."

"Of course it matters. How are you paying your bills?"

"I just told you. By over-drafting."

She shook her head, and then ran her hands across her face and into her hair.

"God, you are going to make me go gray."

I let my head fall back on the pillow.

"Alright," she began again. "I'm going to go see what bail's going to be, and I'll figure it out."

"No, don't do that."

She paused by the door and looked at me. "Excuse me?"

"I don't want your help."

"Well, good thing I never learned to do what men tell me to."

She left the room as the beeping began again, but that time on the hospital monitor.

I didn't want her help. I didn't care what happened to me. I had dug my hole and dragged that piece of shit in it with me. I knew from the assault charge that he wasn't dead. But I was hoping that I had left a lasting impression on him. I was hoping that, after what I'd done and said, it wouldn't be as easy to forget his firstborn daughter.

Natalie was outside on the patio when I came home from the store. She hadn't wanted me to go with her to meet with Edwin. She said I would be too intimidating. I didn't disagree, but I didn't like it.

I set the groceries on the counter and walked to the back patio. She had a glass of wine in her hands, and she was back in her leggings and a long tank top.

"So, how'd it go?" I asked.

She turned her head slightly my way. "Fine," she replied.

But the cracking of her voice told me otherwise. And the tears confirmed it.

I walked over and knelt down in front of her. "What happened?"

She tipped back her glass of wine until it was completely empty.

I knew she shouldn't have seen him. That piece of shit didn't deserve her time.

She rested the glass back on her leg, both hands occupied with it as she avoided my eyes. "He didn't show."

My expression shifted.

Didn't show? I hadn't considered that option.

When she first said she was going to set something up, I was certain he would say no, or at the very least not return her call. But when he had, and he had agreed to see her, this was not an outcome I had thought about.

"He knows I'm dying. I told him that in my original message."

I swallowed a lump.

She was shedding tears for him.

I had seen her shed enough for him for one lifetime.

"What's his address?" I asked, getting to my feet.

"Leo, stop. You're not going to do shit to him," she stated.

"Why the hell not? He deserves it."

"Because I don't need my husband spending my last few months on this earth in jail."

I sighed. "Noted."

She grabbed my hand and pulled me back to her. "Maybe this was the answer I was looking for. It hurts, but at least I know how he feels."

I leaned over, putting my forehead on hers.

She deserved better. He deserved nothing, except maybe a fist to the face. But I also didn't want my remaining time with her full of court appearances and jail time.

"Alright, I secured your bail. They're still going to transfer you to the jail to process the paperwork, but I'll be there to pick you up after."

"I didn't need your fucking help," I said coldly.

"If you didn't want my help, why did you give them my number?"

"I didn't give shit to anyone. I wasn't even conscious until you got here."

"They said you had a note in your wallet to call Diane."

My brows furrowed as I looked to the side of the bed, my wallet lying open.

A card sat on top of it.

"If arrested, please call Diane," I read out loud.

Diane laughed.

It was Natalie's handwriting.

"Watching out for you even from the grave."

I didn't return her smile.

"Oh come on, that's a little funny," she said.

"Well, she knew he had it coming."

"Who?" she asked, her smile disappearing.

"It doesn't matter," I replied, shaking my head. "Do what you need to do. I'll make sure your card stays out of my wallet from now on."

Diane's smile disappeared as she left the room.

***

I was brought to the jail and processed like Diane had said, but before the actual move to the cell, the bail went through and I was released.

Diane was in the front lobby when I walked out. It was 8am and I had only slept during my blackout. If one could call that sleeping. I was starting to feel a hangover set in. Something I hadn't had to experience in months since the hair of the dog was waiting for me each morning.

Diane didn't say anything to me when I reached her. She just turned and walked out the door. I followed her.

I just needed a ride to my car, and then I wouldn't need her help again.

"Your car was impounded. We can get it later today."

Fuck. Maybe I could just Uber there.

"With what money?"

Did Uber take cash? What was left of the drinking money? Maybe I would just walk. But how would I afford to get it out of impound?

"The man you assaulted is out of the hospital."

That was disappointing. Not even a full day in the hospital? I wasn't as tough as I thought.

"Aggravated assault and he doesn't even get a whole day in the hospital?"

"Aggravated assault has less to do with what was inflicted and more to do with the *why* and your overall intentions of it."

I nodded.

"Speaking of which, you wanna dish on who this man is to you?"

"Nope."

She rolled her eyes.

"You're a stubborn asshole."

"That's what I'm told."

"You weren't always though."

"I didn't always have a dead wife."

She exhaled. "You know at some point that's not going to garner you any sympathy."

"I'm not looking for sympathy."

"Then what are you looking for?" she asked, glancing at me briefly and then back at the road.

"To be left alone."

***

Diane was granting my wish and leaving me alone. But I had a feeling it wasn't for good. She had rifled through my mail and took some of it with her. If it wasn't already opened, I would have claimed mail fraud, even though I had no idea how that worked.

By the end of the night, I was dangerously close to the end of my alcohol supply. I was going to have to start pawning stuff from my place. Who cared? They'd take my house within the year anyway.

There was a knock at the door as I dropped the empty glass bottle into the trash.

"Wow, you really are an asshole. You can't even recycle anymore?"

I rolled my eyes.

I was the one who got us recycling. Little Miss had no high horse to sit on.

I opened the front door, surprised to see Ned in all his bruised and bandaged glory.

"One night of pain wasn't enough for you either, huh?" I asked. "Guess we're both just gluttons for punishment."

I couldn't read his expression, but it didn't change with my comment.

Maybe he was there to kill me. That would be a welcomed plot twist.

"I know who you are," he finally said.

"At least we're on even footing now."

"You could have told me yesterday when you dropped off your computer."

I crossed my arms and leaned up against my door frame. "I didn't lie. I gave you my name and number."

"Yeah, but I didn't know who you were."

"Hmm, don't you think it's weird a father-in-law doesn't know his son-in-law's name?"

"You're not my son-in-law, because she's not my daughter."

Nerves briefly coursed through my veins. I knew Natalie's dad went by the nickname Ned now instead of Edwin, but had I gotten the wrong guy?

He must have sensed my confusion, possibly my worry.

"She *was* my daughter," he continued. "But I gave up the right to be her father years ago."

"So, when she called you last year, you thought you would double down and break her heart twice?"

He winced as the words left my mouth.

"That wasn't my intention."

"Then what *was* your intention, *Edwin*?" I asked, stepping onto my porch with him.

His body tensed. I was sure the bruises I had left pulsed in pain with his heartbeat.

"I wanted to see her, but I got worried. I was scared of what she would say to me. I didn't want to hear how terrible of a person I was before she died. Things have already been hard enough for me."

I exhaled, while my head shook. My wrist beeped again.

He swallowed hard as he eyed it.

Maybe it *was* a Leo alarm.

"So you stood her up instead?" I asked.

"Initially—then after a while I felt bad, so I went to the restaurant. But she had already left—"

"—For someone that works with computers, surely you're aware that phones exist."

He nodded, looking down at his feet. "I tried. But I couldn't bring myself to call."

"She died thinking she did something to make her dad not love her."

His eyes shot up to mine. "I loved her."

"No, you didn't," I said, shaking my head. "*I* loved her. You know how I know the difference? *I* was here."

"I left *for* her. It was better that way. When I got Martha pregnant, I was scared—"

"—Seems to be a trend with you, *Ned*."

"Teresa was already done with me. Martha was going to leave if I didn't marry her. She wanted to make our family work. I didn't want to lose another shot at it."

"You're a coward," I said. "You missed out on knowing the best human I've ever known."

He nodded, keeping his eyes from me. After a moment, he shuffled the backpack off his shoulder that I hadn't even noticed. He carefully set it on the ground and unzipped it.

I half expected him to pull out a gun. It wasn't like I had delivered on any type of apologies for my previous night's actions. Nor would I. Even with a barrel to the temple.

When his hand came back out, my computer was in it.

"I got it to turn back on," he said.

My eyes went wide. Not because he was *able* to fix it, but because he *had*.

He swallowed hard as he handed me the computer. "It appears you mostly just had pictures saved on there. I would get them backed up soon, just in case it fails you again."

I stayed silent, staring at the piece of technology in my hands that held six years' worth of memories I hadn't had access to in almost a decade.

"I didn't look through them," he continued. "I just saw the screen saver." The ends of his bruised and beaten lips curled into a smile. "She was a beautiful bride."

Our wedding photos. Luckily the photographer had had duplicates of those.

"Yeah, she was," I replied, feeling tears well up in my eyes.

Where was my anger? I wanted that back.

"I'm glad she got the life she deserved," he said, his eyes briefly meeting mine. "Thank you for loving her."

Chapter Nine
{Sunday, May 20th, 2018}

My feet hit the pavement in quick succession. My breathing was steady, rhythmic. The air around me had a chill—but it was still early.

A lack of sleep had brought me back to my morning jogs. I hated them without her. I hated everything. That was apparent.

I stopped, putting my hands on my knees. I was out of shape. Undoubtedly because I hadn't run in almost a year. The bottle of Jack every day didn't help.

My phone buzzed in my pocket.

It had just been turned back on the night before. Diane had gotten the insurance company to pay out the amount they weren't disputing while she tried to work out the rest. Lucky for me, it covered enough to catch up all my past bills. Although that was it.

Unfortunately, I would need to start selling stuff as my bank instituted a new limit on overdrafts. Guess all my years banking with them meant nothing next to the amount of debt I had gone into.

I shifted up and pulled the phone out of my pocket. My mom had left a message.

I clicked on it, and continued on, walking instead of running.

"Well, I'm happy I'm at least getting your voicemail this time. The last two times I got a message saying you couldn't receive calls. Is everything okay? Why couldn't you receive calls? Grant said it would say that if you didn't pay your bills? Why aren't you paying your bills? You missed last week's phone call. If you miss this week's, I'm going to take that as a sign that you need me to come stay with you. Please call me. I love you."

The message ended as I clicked the side and put it back into my pocket, picking up my speed once more.

I was happy I didn't have to wear the monitor to track my blood pressure anymore. I should've been on medication, but I opted out. I promised to try to manage my stress levels instead. Jogging early in the morning was me trying.

Ms. Bates blew the whistle, bringing gym class to an end. Natalie said something to one of her friends but didn't walk with them. Instead she waited for me.

I took her hand in mine and kissed it.

"You looked good out there today," I said, rubbing my thumb against her sweaty palms.

"Me? I couldn't keep my eyes off of you in those basketball shorts."

"These old things?" I asked, with a smirk.

"Just the two I wanted to see," Ms. Bates said as we stepped into the hallway.

She eyed our hands, more than likely hoping we would separate, but we didn't.

"What's wrong?" Natalie asked.

"Listen, I know you two are dating, but you know the rules."

I raised my brow. There were dating rules? What class did we learn that in? Was that in the handbook? I'd never read it.

"Rules?" I asked.

She nodded. "You are not to be kissing on school premises."

"Are you serious?" I asked.

Natalie squeezed my hand.

"Sorry, I just mean, everyone kisses in school."

"Maybe, but they weren't caught."

"Caught? I haven't even kissed her since before class."

"Well, one, that's not helping, and two, I wasn't talking about today."

"So we're in trouble for past kissing?"

She was getting frustrated with me.

"You're not in trouble—yet. But if you are caught again, you will be."

"I don't even know how you caught us this time."

She handed me the piece of paper I hadn't even noticed in her hand.

It was a black and white printout of Natalie's and my silhouettes locking lips.

It was art.

"I'm sorry, Ms. Bates. It won't happen again," Natalie said.

Ms. Bates remained silent, waiting for the same assurance from me.

I looked up when the silence stayed firm.

"Oh, yeah. Sorry, we won't ever kiss again."

Natalie checked me with her hip.

I laughed. "I mean, at school."

Ms. Bates put her hand out for the paper.

"Uh, can I keep this?" I asked.

Her brows furrowed. "You want it?"

I nodded.

"I guess," she replied before walking away.

"Well, I think we need to quit school," I said to Natalie after our teachers' departure.

"Why?"

"They expect me to go each day without kissing you. That's absurd."

"It'll be torture," she mocked.

"I won't survive."

"Even if I promise to make it up to you after school each day?"

I paused. "Every day? Immediately after?"

"Yup. And just think about all the built-up sexual frustration I'll have to unleash once we're home."

I swallowed hard. "I'd rather not be thinking of any of that right now since I'm about to go into a locker room you're not allowed into."

"Oh, shit, sorry. Yeah, don't think about that now."

I wanted to kiss her, but I knew if Ms. Bates wasn't watching, the cameras certainly were.

I put my hand out.

She raised her brow.

"Well, I can't kiss you, so we'll have to settle for a handshake."

She laughed as she put her hand in mine and shook it.

"Love you," I said, as if we had just completed a transaction.

She shook her head as her smile grew. "I love you, too."

My throat hurt. The air I was breathing in felt like fire.

How fast had I been running? And how long?

I again put my hands on my knees, doing my best to catch my breath.

Once I did, I glanced around. My eyes narrowed as I tried to make sense of my whereabouts.

I stared at the big brick building that sat about 30 feet from where I stood. Why had I stopped there? Was it because the walkway resembled the one back home? Was the brickwork familiar? Had my subconscious led me there or was it a coincidence?

I pushed my hand into my side, trying to relieve the pain. Too bad I couldn't do the same for my heart.

I stood in front of the few steps that led up to the main walkway. Before I knew it, I was moving in that direction. The trees lining the path looked like something I would design. Maybe I had. Certainly I would have remembered that though.

My feet stopped just shy of the next set of stairs. I glanced up. The brickwork looked aged. But many of these older buildings, while structurally sound, did have a tendency of showing their history.

I sighed. What was I doing? I ran my hand through my hair, and then started to turn around. The sound of the large door opening stopped me.

"Can I help you?" a man asked.

I hadn't planned on speaking to anyone. Besides my limited forced communication with Diane, and the poor bank teller the week before, I hadn't talked to anyone in at least two weeks.

"No," I finally managed to say.

"Church doesn't start for another two hours."

I nodded. Certainly I didn't look like I was there for the service.

He was gathering as much, probably just being nice.

"Do you want to come in?" he asked.

I shook my head. "No, sorry for disturbing you."

He walked the few steps down to me in quick succession before I got too far.

"Hey," he said, causing me to turn to him.

"Something brought you here," he said, like it was a fact.

"Yeah, my feet," I retorted and again began my walk.

He reached out and grabbed my arm.

He was bold.

"Sorry," he said, after seeing my expression.

I was terrifying these days.

"How about you come in and rest for a minute?"

Did I look like I needed to rest? Or did I look like I needed a pep talk? I nodded regardless.

He motioned with his hand for me to lead the way. Maybe it was because he half expected me to book it as soon as he turned back around.

Maybe I would've.

He shut the large door, the sound echoing through the sanctuary. I glanced around. The inside looked new. Nothing like the outside.

"Have you ever been?" he asked, moving to stand next to me, looking with me at the high ceilings and brightly painted walls.

"No."

I saw him nod from the corner of my eye.

Why was he talking to me? Was it minister guilt? Pastor? Priest? Whatever they were called.

"What are you?" I asked.

It took him a minute to understand my question.

"I'm the pastor," he replied. "I moved here with my family a few months ago."

I nodded.

"Are you a member of another church?"

I shook my head.

"Have you been to church before?"

I shook my head again. "But I got married in one."

He nodded, his smile growing. "Is the wife religious then?"

I shrugged. "She was confused."

He smiled.

I hadn't expected that at my answer.

"Many are."

I nodded, grimacing at his remark. "I think I rested long enough," I began, turning to head back to the door.

"I have a feeling you haven't rested in a while."

Was it that obvious? Or was that just pastor bullshit?

"I just ran a lot further than I anticipated this morning."

"Maybe there was a reason for that."

"Maybe."

"Why don't you have a seat? Just for a few."

"I'm fine, really."

"Please don't take this the wrong way," he began. "But you don't look fine."

"Well, you don't look like a pastor."

He laughed.

Again, I hadn't expected that.

"Fair enough," he said. "But even still, sit—at least for a few. I have to go get the coffee started for the choir folks or we might have more yawns than high C's," he continued, chuckling to himself.

I didn't share in his delight, but I did sit.

He was satisfied with that, disappearing out of the room to make the coffee.

He must have turned on more lights from where he was. Either that or God—Jesus, whoever, whatever—was communicating with me.

The light beamed on over the front of the sanctuary where the pastor, bride, and groom would stand to say their vows. Two rings. Two sets of vows. One kiss. A sealed deal 'til death do you part.

A deal I had been certain would be much longer.

"Nervous?" Mark asked, his hand slapping my back.

"About the marriage? No. Standing in front of all these people? Absolutely."

172

He laughed as we looked in at the seated crowd waiting for the ceremony to begin.

My mom spotted me just on the other side of the doors and winked. I smiled back.

Mark and Grant stood by me, waiting for Beth and Diane to come out.

Mark looked more natural in a suit than my teenage brother. Grant would look even younger walking with Beth. I smirked. He was excited for it.

I got the nod from my aunt who was keeping everything running smoothly.

Show time.

I took a deep breath and looked at Mark.

"Go get 'em, Tiger," he said.

I exhaled. "That was weak."

"Well, that's all you get," he replied with a laugh.

I shook my head as he put his arms out and pulled me to him.

I almost didn't have time to react before he was moving me away from him in the same manner.

"That was—unexpected," I said.

"Yeah, well, I'm overcome with emotions. Now go get married."

I nodded and walked through the door and down the aisle to my spot.

Tim McGraw's "My Best Friend" flowed from the speakers as Beth walked in, arm tucked around Grant's. Both smiling. Surely for different reasons.

I smirked.

Diane and Mark came next. They complimented each other well. Something I was sure didn't sit well with Beth as she and Mark had just started dating.

I expected Natalie to be upset about her friend dating Mark, but she liked that we had a couple to double date with. Plus she said Mark was more bearable to be around when he was dating someone. I didn't disagree.

Mark lightly bumped my shoulder as he passed me, bringing my attention to him for a brief moment before a shimmer of white caught my eye.

My gaze fell on the stunning woman that stood in the doorway.

My eyes widened, peering directly into hers.

Teresa's arm was linked with Natalie's, walking her towards me. My excitement rose with every step.

I walked down the few steps to her, not wanting to wait any longer to be beside her.

Teresa and Natalie laughed.

"God, you look—" I began.

"—I believe the word you're looking for is gorgeous."

I smiled at the reference. But just like back then, gorgeous didn't begin to describe her.

"You got her, kid?" Teresa asked me.

"Until the day I die," I replied.

Teresa nodded in approval and kissed Natalie's cheek. "I love you, baby girl."

Natalie wrapped her arms around her mom. "I love you, Mom."

Teresa wiped her tears and walked to her seat.

I extended my hand to Natalie. "You got about two minutes before it's too late to run," I whispered.

"Two minutes, you say?" she whispered back, as if she was considering it. "Sorry, no dice," she said with a smile as she took my hand. "You're stuck with me."

The pastor dropped something up front, bringing me back from one of the best days of my life.

His expression showed his remorse at interrupting me.

He walked up to the podium and flipped open a book. Probably a Bible. He took a stack of papers and tapped them on the wood, then looked at me.

"Do you mind if I test my opening on you?"

My brows furrowed. I glanced around to see if someone else, maybe another worker from the church had entered. But no one had. He was talking to me.

"I guess," I replied from the second-to-last pew.

He adjusted the microphone and looked down at his papers. He was silent for what seemed like minutes, but probably wasn't. Time had been lost to me in recent months.

I put my arms on the pew in front of me and leaned my head on them. Intent on listening but wanting nothing to do with responding to his sermon.

"So many people walk around with a meaningless life," he began, my head shooting up at the sound of the familiar words.

He continued as I sat completely still, watching him speak. "They seem half-asleep, even when they're busy doing things they think are important. This is because they're chasing the wrong things."

I joined in his quoting of one of my favorite books.

After a few lines, he stopped. Either because he was done quoting *Tuesdays with Morrie*, or because he had seen me doing it too.

"That's Mitch Albom," I said as I stood up.

He nodded and then smiled. "It is, yes."

What the fuck was happening?

"I thought you only quoted the Bible here."

He smiled. "I often do, but not all the time."

"Why did you pick that one?"

"I'm a fan," he replied with a shrug. "Why? Are you not?"

I walked towards the front slowly.

"I am. Or I used to be anyway."

"Used to be?" he asked, one of his brows rising to his forehead wrinkles.

"I just don't believe it anymore."

"Believe what?"

"What I used to—what he wrote."

"What? About life having meaning?"

"Yeah."

"You don't think there's meaning to life?"

"Not anymore," I said.

"Why is that?"

"It's hard to find meaning in death."

"How so?"

I exhaled, annoyed by his question. "What's the point of any of it, if you just get sick and die?"

"The point is to enjoy it while you're here. As Mitch wrote, devote yourself to loving others, devote yourself to your comm—"

"—I devoted myself to loving someone and look where that got me," I interjected.

"Where are you?" he asked after a brief pause.

"Huh?"

"Where is it you are? Where did it get you?"

I sighed. "It brought me to a place I never imagined I could be."

"And that is?"

"A world without her."

His face held an expression I couldn't quite read. But I saw him swallow and then he walked to me.

"What do you believe happens when people die?"

I shrugged. I genuinely didn't know.

He nodded, like he understood. But how could he? He was a pastor and had his faith in his God.

"I already know what you believe," I began. "I already know about heaven."

"That's all fine and dandy, but it's not comforting if you don't actually believe in it."

He wasn't wrong. The thought didn't bring me comfort, because even if it did exist, I still had to wait God-knows-how-long until I got to join her.

He took a deep breath and sat in the front pew next to where I stood.

Not wanting to tower over him, I followed suit.

I wasn't sure if he was thinking of what to say to me that was comforting, or was waiting for me to speak, but regardless, I did.

"So if the way to get meaning into your life is to devote yourself to loving others, and to a relationship that gives you purpose, what does it all mean when that person dies?"

My body was tensed up next to his.

"The quote talks about loving others and community. You can't resign yourself to only loving one person."

"As a pastor, you really shouldn't encourage infidelity," I joked.

Doing so felt foreign to my body.

He rolled his eyes, but smirked. "Friends and family. Others to love. Others to *be* loved by. You can't put all your eggs in one basket."

I chuckled, but it was hollow. "Where were you when I found the love of my life at 16?"

He sighed.

We both heard the hurt in my tone.

"When did she pass?"

I swallowed a lump. "Last September."

He nodded, his expression sympathetic, a look I knew well.

"Ya know," he began. "Comforting words are only comforting if the person wants to be comforted."

"And you don't think I do?"

His lip raised on one side, but it wasn't a smile, just remnants of his sympathy.

"I think you are looking for logic in an illogical situation."

"No, I'm looking for a time machine. Or at the very least, someone to make a deal with."

"Only the devil makes deals."

I chuckled, but it wasn't out of laughter. "Well, then, I'm in the wrong place."

I was expecting him to throw me out. I wasn't trying to be a jackass. I was just telling the truth. I would sell my soul for Natalie to be alive again.

"I'm sorry," I finally said in his silence.

"There's nothing to be sorry for. Making deals, or wanting to anyway, is a part of the grieving process."

"Jim," a woman said. "Oh, I'm sorry to interrupt."

"It's okay," I said, getting to my feet.

"You don't have to go," Pastor Jim said.

"Thank you for letting me rest. I'm good now," I replied, attempting a friendly nod at the woman.

Before he could continue, I walked out of the sanctuary, pulling the large door shut behind me.

I took a deep breath before preparing for my run—walk—home.

The sky was bright blue with random spots of white. It made everything look as though it was the same. Like the earth and my existence wasn't as dark as it felt.

"I haven't done this whole praying thing since I was a kid, so I'm sure I'm not very good at it." I was talking out loud, essentially to myself. If anyone saw me, they would think I was crazy. And maybe I was.

"Jim said you don't make deals. So, this is kind of pointless, I guess. But on the off chance you do, I want you to know that, if you change this, if you change what happened to Natalie, if you make this all just be a bad dream—if you somehow bring her back to life—I would be the best person on this earth—Gandhi would have nothing on me."

I laughed. It was dumb.

But the laughter and my stupid jokes were just to help repress my tears.

"Please, I'm begging you. I'm begging the universe. Don't let this be it. I don't know how to exist without her."

***

Why are photo albums a thing?

Why do people take the time to print out all the pictures and then not even put them in frames on the wall?

Instead, they make the conscious decision to put the pictures into books that you may never look at again. Or at least not until someone dies.

Was that what they were for? Death? To look at and remember the happier days?

That seems like morbid thinking. Preparing these books for when someone is gone.

But regardless of Natalie's intention, she had created them. She had bought specific papers, stickers, and a hot glue gun. She was super into scrapbooking for about a year. Then we got busy. Maybe depressed. Most likely both.

Maybe she didn't want to document the lack of kids in our life. Though that was something she had seemed to come to terms with a few years earlier.

I opened up a scrapbook she had made for me. Or more accurately *of* me. She had a lot of pictures left over from the wedding that my mother had given us to use. She was more than happy to let Natalie keep them when she asked.

I glanced at the front picture. A goofy-looking baby in a tub. A popular setup I hadn't planned on duplicating with my kids.

Most of the book was me as a baby and toddler. That meant Grant wasn't in many, as he wasn't born until a few months before my fifth birthday.

The second-to-last page held the picture of the first time I held him. I was so excited. My mom said I cried. I had always wanted a brother. I asked them all the time for one. Mom said other kids were asking for pets. But me? I wanted a sibling.

Although the photo album didn't show the full story, there weren't many pictures after he was born that didn't contain the two of us. At least in our younger years. We were inseparable. Even with the age gap.

I sighed and shut the book. I didn't want to be thinking of him. I felt I had successfully moved through the anger phase but thinking of him had the potential of bringing me back to it.

Picking up the fifth of Jack at my side, I finished the last swig before lining it against similar empty bottles.

I maneuvered onto my feet from the floor and stared at the pile of photo albums and pictures that were about to take up space in my junk closet. Well, at least until the inevitable foreclosure of the house.

I picked up the books and placed them into an empty tote, tossing the photos in with it.

Lifting the tote, I headed to the stairs and started up. As I reached the top, I miscalculated the step, slipped, and fell down the stairs, photos and books flying through the air.

God, it hurt. Everywhere. But the pain wasn't searing, so I assumed no broken bones. Maybe that would be different when I tried to stand. But I was in no rush to move. I could lie there for days and, unless Diane decided to stop by and annoy the fuck out of me, no one would notice.

I was fine with that. With being alone. At least I didn't have to put on a show for anyone. I didn't have to pretend to be okay. Pretend to be sober. Pretend to be the same Leo that had been buried with my wife the year before.

"Get up, babe."

"Why?" I asked.

But that was pointless; she wouldn't respond. It wasn't her telling me things. It was my drunken state of mind playing tricks on me.

I closed my eyes, prepared to pass out right there at the bottom of the steps. It was as good of a place as any. Sleep was sleep, right? Even if it was Jack-induced.

"Where do you think I'll go when I die?" Natalie asked as we lay on a blanket in our backyard.

The sun had just set, and we were lying in the dark, holding each other while we could.

"I imagine you'll go where all the angels go."

She nudged me with her hip. "Shut up."

"What? That was a sweet answer."

"That was a cop-out answer."

"Okay, you're right," I replied with a laugh. "You're a pretty shitty human, so I'm guessing you'll burn in the fiery pits of hell."

She laughed, which I was relieved for. Because while I laughed too, the thought of even the possibility of her being in misery caused my chest to seize up.

"I see I'm not going to get a legit answer out of you."

"Probably not," I replied, turning on my side to face her.

She sighed and continued to stare up at the sky. "What if there's nothing after death?"

I had no words to comfort her. I didn't know what I believed. And that wouldn't be comforting. But not saying anything wasn't comforting either.

I didn't respond to her question, and she didn't follow up.

After a few minutes of her looking at the night sky, and me looking at her, I finally spoke. "What do you want there to be?"

She turned her head towards me. "What?"

"What do you want to happen after death?"

She gazed into my eyes for a moment, thinking hard about her answer. But then she turned and glanced back up at the black void. "I want to be a ghost. That way I can still be with you—hang around the house, leaving cupboard doors open, and turning lights on and off. Maybe I could show up in the mirror when you say my name three times."

My eyes narrowed as I smirked. "You wanna be Bloody Mary?"

She laughed. "Maybe just a nicer version."

"So you won't stab me if you show up in my bathroom mirror?"

"Nah, I'll just cover you in kisses instead."

"That's the weirdest haunting I've ever heard of."

"Is it haunting if you're just wanting to be with the person?"

I shrugged. "Whatever it's called, I'm okay with it. But you're going to have to figure out a way to communicate."

"Hopefully they have a how-to-haunt class or, at the very least, a guidebook."

"If they're any good at their jobs, they will."

We both smirked as I rolled on to my back and she snuggled up, resting her head on my chest.

"Honestly, I don't care where I go as long as I still get to see you."

"That seems a little one sided. I want to be where I can see you too."

She draped her arm over my midsection and held me tight. "Can I ask you a favor?"

"No."

"No?" she asked, lifting her head to look at me.

I returned the look and laughed. "Knowing you and this conversation, it's going to be something I can't honor."

"You don't know that."

"Is it?"

"Of course it is," she replied with a laugh.

I shook my head in disbelief. "Alright, ask away."

She exhaled and put her head back on my chest. "Can you keep your grieving period to one year?"

My brows furrowed. I looked at her once more, but she didn't look at me. "You want me to have a time clock on my grief?"

She nodded, her head rubbing against my chest.

"I mean, I can try, but I promise nothing."

"Like you'll try-try, or are you just saying that?"

"I'm just saying that."

She playfully hit my stomach.

"What? I can't guarantee something like that."

"Well, if you don't, then I will show up in the bathroom with a knife."

She laughed, and I smiled.

"Whatever it takes to see you again," I replied before we both went silent.

Were all our conversations going to end like that? On a sad note?

I gripped her body a little tighter, pushing her up against me, knowing I couldn't give her the guarantee she was looking for.

"Leo!" I heard.

It may have come after a knock. Maybe a few.

"Leo!" I heard again through the front door.

I tipped my head back, looking at Grant through my front window.

Why was he upside-down?

I moved my head to look straight up. I was staring at the ceiling.

I had forgotten about the fall. How long had I been asleep? Had I slept? Or had I passed out?

"If you don't let me in, I'll break down the door," he yelled through the glass.

I sighed.

I didn't want to get up. It was actually kind of nice just lying there. Dreaming of her. Not being in my current realm. My daydreams were the best part of my days.

I rolled on to my side and slowly but surely got to my feet. Grant gawked through the window the entire time.

I unlocked the front door and pulled on the knob.

"Jesus Christ, man, you scared the shit out of me," he said, storming in the minute the door was opened.

"Sorry, I missed a step at the top and fell," I explained.

"Are you okay?"

"It didn't kill me," I replied, clearly disappointed.

His demeanor shifted to what it had been at Christmas. "Oh, sweet. Still riding the Leo pity party."

"Seems like it. Which begs the question, if you aren't looking to join in, why are you here?"

"You didn't call Mom back."

"I was busy."

"Doing what?"

"Seeing a man about a horse."

His eyes narrowed, and I chuckled to myself.

"Do you need to get checked for a concussion?"

I sighed and walked past him.

He shut the door and then followed behind as I headed into the kitchen.

"Listen, just report back to Mom that I'm alive and all is well," I said, reaching for the Jack and taking off the cap.

"You're alive, but I wouldn't say all is well."

"That's subjective."

"What are you doing, Leo?"

"What are *you* doing, Grant? Why are you here, in my house? Clearly you would rather be anywhere else."

"I overstayed my welcome at Mom's."

"Well, you've overstayed your welcome here, too."

"Nope, you broke your deal with Mom, so now you get a roommate again."

I shook my head. "I don't need a watchdog."

"No, clearly you need a padded cell, but Mom thought this was a better alternative."

"Yeah, I mean surely if I don't need one now, I will in a week of living with you."

"You think living with me will be bad? No one even likes you anymore. We have to pull straws to see who's checking up on the sad sack."

"Sucks that you finally pulled the short one."

"Yeah, well someone had to take one for the team so that Mom didn't quit her job to be with you."

"She wouldn't do that," I replied with an eye roll. "And I can handle myself."

I took that moment to put the open bottle of Jack to my lips and let at least a shot's worth run down the back of my throat.

"Looks like all you're taking care of is the local liquor store."

"Someone's got to keep 'em in business. I figure, why not me?"

He didn't respond.

He was already sick of my shit. There was no way he was going to make it a week.

I picked up the bottle and walked towards the living room. I paused just inside the doorway and turned to Grant. "Well, if you insist on subjecting yourself to all this, then be my guest. But the couch is mine."

Chapter Ten
{Thursday, June 7th, 2018}

"Grant's fine, Mom," I said in an exhale over the phone.

"Are the two of you getting along?"

"As much as two people in forced cohabitation can be."

"Leo," she replied sternly.

"Yes, Mother?"

I could feel her scolding stare through the phone.

"Listen, Mom, he's here. I'm here. We haven't killed each other. It'll be fine. But you need to stop calling every day. Isn't that the point of him being here?"

She sighed. She was conceding.

"This is a great opportunity for the two of you to get to know each other again. Try not to squander it."

I wanted to say that we knew each other just fine. But I had been arguing with her since he had arrived two weeks before. I was going to take the newest conversation as a win.

"Mom, I need to go make breakfast. I'll call you next weekend."

"And what will happen if you don't?" she asked.

"You will show up on my doorstep like Grant did."

"Sure will," she replied matter-of-factly. "I love you, Leo."

"I love you too, Mom."

I clicked end and set my phone down on the coffee table in front of me.

"We're out of food," Grant said, walking into the living room.

Those were the first words he had said to me in the past week. The ones before that were "you're out of booze."

That one I was a lot quicker about rectifying.

"So, go get some," I replied bitterly.

"I don't know what me living in my parents' house said, but I'm broke."

"Well," I responded, laying my head on my pillow. "Join the club."

"Yeah, I have noticed a lack of leaving for work these days."

"At least you still have a keen sense of observation."

He sat on the arm of the chair across the room, trying to read me.

His constant back and forth was more fucking annoying than Diane's unannounced check-ins. Judging by the few weeks it had been since I had seen her, she was due back any day.

"Have you not gone to work because of me being here?" he asked, looking more like my little brother than he had in the past few years. It was nice to see him without anger, or attitude, in his eyes.

"Yes. I couldn't very well just leave you home with my valuables all day."

He stood up and rolled his eyes. "What valuables? Looks like you've pawned a good amount of your shit."

"If you know I'm pawning stuff, then what the fuck did you expect me to do about food?"

He shrugged. "Pawn something so we can *eat*."

"Well, I'm not hungry, and you're a grown-ass man. Figure it out."

I rolled onto my side and faced the back of the couch.

He stayed for a minute. He probably had something to add. Color me shocked that he didn't.

His footsteps receded from the room and up the stairs, back to one of the two guest bedrooms we had. The room he had picked as his fortress of solitude. It was the farthest away from my wing of the house. It was best for both of us. Well, unless he was hungry anyway.

I stared at the back of my eyelids, and then the back of the couch. I was tired. But I was always tired. Being tired never equated to sleep for me.

I exhaled frustratedly as I moved to sit on the edge of the couch.

He was a 27-year-old man. He could find his own food.

That's what I kept repeating in my head.

But my own thoughts were being drowned out by Natalie's.

"Just go buy some food for the house. You're going to need to eat, too."

I ran my hand through my hair and then along the scruff that had turned into a very untamed beard.

I glanced down at my clothes, pulling my shirt to my nose.

It was bad that the sniff test had gotten entirely too lenient. I needed to put it down a notch if I was going out in public.

But did I? Was I trying to impress anyone? I just needed food. Well, Grant needed food.

I sighed. Why was I suddenly responsible for the well-being of two grown men?

"This was your mom's plan all along."

It probably was.

I stood up, grabbed my keys, phone, and wallet from the coffee table, and shut the front door behind me.

Once in my car, I started the ignition and looked at the gas gauge. Empty. I laughed.

Of course it was.

I turned it off and walked back in the house up to Grant's room.

"Shit, you can use the stairs successfully?" he asked as I stood in the doorway to the room.

"I need your keys. I'm outta gas."

"So get gas."

I exhaled, trying not to be more of a dick than I had been. "I barely have enough money for food. Do you want me to spend it on gas? Or do you just want to loan me your car?"

He shook his head and tossed me his keys. "You're supposed to be the responsible one, you know."

"Well, looks like there's a spot to be filled. Feel free to do so," I retorted before turning and heading back down the stairs.

***

Being almost broke meant Walmart instead of Whole foods. I really didn't mind. Food was food. Natalie was more of a food snob than I was. I just always ate fancier things because she liked it.

I grabbed a basket from the front and walked to the frozen meal section. Grant wasn't a cook; neither was I. Frozen meals seemed the most appropriate both cost and skill-wise.

When I reached the aisle, I looked around, trying to find the cheapest ones.

"I just need some ice cream for my niece's party," a woman said into her phone as she walked down the aisle, doing the same scan of the food.

But she was in the wrong aisle.

"No, I just stopped at Walmart. I'm heading over there right after."

I glanced over at her, seeing she now noticed that she was in the entirely wrong section.

Her long hair ran down her shoulders, covering the parts of her chest that her tank top didn't. Her dark blue jeans swayed with her hips and her heels clicked on the ground.

"God, I need to get out of this fucking store," she said into the phone as she side-eyed me.

I had been staring.

Why the fuck was I staring?

"Because she was pretty."

Natalie's comment hit even harder since I knew it wasn't her at all, and just my subconscious.

An ache pierced my chest; my blood pressure was certainly skyrocketing. That was either from the fact I just saw a woman I found attractive, or because I instantly felt like the worst person in the world for thinking she was.

Regardless, I was nervous about the clean-up in the frozen food section I would cause when the nosebleed came.

I opened the door in front of the Michelina's frozen meals and put as many boxes as I could into the basket before booking it out of the aisle.

***

When I got to Grant's car, I tossed the bags in the back and got into the driver's seat. I started the ignition and then leaned my head against the steering wheel, gripping it with both hands.

What the fuck was that? How could I look at another woman? What the fuck was wrong with me?

I was still grieving Natalie. It hadn't even been a year.

"It's been a year since you last had sex or, ya know, handled things yourself."

Had it been a whole year already?

I exhaled as I tried to calm my thoughts.

Natalie's legs were on either side of my head, my tongue's movement caused her to tug on my hair. I could hear her moans from above the blanket. She needed to be quiet, or we would wake her mom, but God did I want to keep hearing her.

I pulled my head away and shifted to look at her from under the blanket.

"You need to be quiet," I said with a smirk.

She took a deep breath and glanced down at me. "I'm fucking trying. You're making it really hard."

"Pretty sure you're the one making it hard," I quipped.

She giggled, and bit her bottom lip, moving her hands to my arms and pulling me up to her.

194

"I want you," she whispered when my face was an inch away from hers.

"You have me," I replied.

She laughed. "I mean, I want to have sex with you."

I swallowed hard. There was no doubt I wanted that too.

"Here on your love seat?" I asked.

"Isn't that what they're for?"

"Not in your bed?"

"Right next to my mom's room?"

I shifted to sit beside her on the couch. "Good point."

"I love you, Leo," she said.

"Are you sure?" I asked.

Her brows furrowed.

I smiled. "I mean, are you sure about having sex with me?"

Her expression relaxed. "Absolutely."

There was almost no time between her answer and me moving my lips to hers. Her body shifted with mine to lie on the love seat. Her oversized t-shirt and my boxer briefs were the only articles of clothing still on us.

"Do you have a condom?" she asked, breathlessly.

"Yeah."

I reached for my jeans next to the couch and pulled out my wallet.

"How cliché of you," she said with a smirk.

I kissed her forehead. "Where else would I keep it?"

She shrugged and shifted up underneath me so I could pull down my boxers and put on the protection I had been given as a joke from a friend at school.

I was glad I hadn't just thrown it away.

When the condom was in place, I looked over at her. She was staring. It made me nervous.

"Are you sure you're ready?"

She took a deep breath, letting her eyes meet mine. "Yes."

She smiled, and I returned it with one of my own, putting my hand behind her head and bringing her lips to mine. "I love you," I whispered.

Shifting my body back onto hers, her eyes met mine. "I love you, too."

The long, drawn-out beep stole me away from Natalie and brought me back to the Walmart parking lot.

"Moving anytime soon, buddy?" a man yelled from his truck.

I wanted to yell something back, but I was in no position to fight. I doubted my fists would be as hard as a certain other body part. I didn't need Diane seeing *that* in a police report.

I gave a slight wave, putting the car into reverse. He backed up some, allowing me to get out.

In the future, if Grant was hungry, it would officially not be my problem.

***

"Need any help?" Grant asked from the front door as I pulled the bags out of the back.

"No, I got it."

I shut the door and walked inside.

"Frozen meals?" he said.

"If you want home-cooked meals, go back to Mom's."

"I didn't say I didn't want these."

I rolled my eyes and moved past him to the kitchen.

"How was the outside world?" he asked, joining me as I put away the meals.

"It was a ray of sunshine. Maybe you should try it."

He shrugged, snagging one of the boxes from my grasp. "We'll probably run out of alcohol at some point, so I'll go then for you."

"Great, you'll probably have to go sooner rather than later," I replied gruffly as I shut the freezer and threw the bags on the counter.

"Did something happen?"

"No, I just don't want to run out."

"Would it be so bad to be sober for just a little while?"

"I was sober enough for that trip. I would like to not have to do that again anytime soon."

I opened the fridge and grabbed one of the fifths off the shelf.

"You're going to have to pawn something else if you expect a restock. Shit ain't cheap."

"Why don't *you* pawn something instead of getting a free ride off my shit?"

"Because I don't have anything of value."

I rolled my eyes.

"Whatever. There are rooms full of stuff. Take your pick. Just don't touch the shit in the living room."

He nodded as I walked in the opposite direction of my normal hangout.

"Where are you going?" he asked.

"To shower."

"Do you need the alcohol for that?"

"I need the alcohol for everything."

***

I sat on the edge of the tub having finished half of the fifth. My headache subsided about ten minutes into locking myself in the bathroom, but the need for some release was holding strong.

I leaned over and turned on the shower, letting the air fill with steam until the mirror was cloudy.

I set the bottle on the counter and pulled off my clothes before stepping behind the curtain.

I closed my eyes, letting the scalding water hit my skin.

I knew I should have opted for a cold shower. But I didn't know whether to lean into the need for her, or to resist it. I didn't know if I had the ability to resist the thought of her.

"Good morning, Mrs. Algar," I said to Natalie as her eyes opened, but then immediately regretted it. *"Okay, that's going to take some adjustment."*

She laughed. "Does it help if you call me Mrs. Leo Algar?"

I scrunched up my nose. "Not really. How about I just call you my wife?"

198

She stared lovingly into my eyes. "I love it."

I leaned over and kissed her.

"I'm so sorry I fell asleep last night," she added.

"Were you supposed to pull an all-nighter?" I asked.

"No, I mean, before we could have sex."

I shrugged. "We were both tired. It was a long day."

She nodded, and then shifted her body on top of mine, straddling me.

"I'm not tired now," she said, moving her lips to my chest.

"I can see that."

She giggled as pulled off her tank top and threw it to the floor.

"Fuck, is this real life?" I asked.

"They're just breasts, Leo."

I laughed in unison with her.

"You're perfect," I said.

"You're trying really hard at a sure thing."

I smiled, putting my hands behind her head and guiding her lips to mine.

Her tongue slipped into my mouth as her hands moved from my jaw line down my neck and to my shoulders.

My hands moved to her ass, my fingers running alongside the edge of her underwear. I maneuvered one of my hands between her legs and pushed aside the fabric, sliding my fingers inside of her.

She was already excited for my touch. My thumb moving against her clit made her moans louder.

I shut my eyes, trying to contain myself at the feeling of her.

She shifted beside me, slipping her hand into my boxers and taking me into her grasp.

My chest rose and fell with my low moans.

I opened my eyes to see her watching me—deriving pleasure from what she was doing.

As quickly as one could, I slid down my boxers, ripped off her underwear, and thrusted between her legs.

She moaned loudly, my eyes shutting, taking in the euphoric sound of her pleasure.

My tongue tasted hers, and then moved to her neck.

Her grip on my back tightened as her moans grew louder.

"Should I get one?" I asked, breathlessly.

She didn't open her eyes. "No—"

Fuck, she was too close, but so was I. If I didn't stop now, I wouldn't be able to.

"Babe—" I began, watching as her body tensed up.

"Fuck—" she exclaimed, wrapping her legs around me, as I continued to thrust into her. "Don't stop. Don't stop," she continued.

And as she dug her nails into my back, I came in unison with her.

The water poured over me, dick in hand. But as badly as I needed to finish, I found myself just as close to crying as I did to coming.

I let my hand drop, more frustrated than I'd ever been.

Maybe it was whisky dick.

"Maybe you should try jerking off to something less depressing."

Memories of the first time I had sex with my wife were beautiful. But I would never fuck her again. All I had left were memories. Apparently, memories I couldn't even get off to.

How fucking sad was that?

***

I cooked one of my frozen dinners and took it into the living room. It was dark out, but I used the light of the TV to see my food.

I hadn't been an avid TV watcher since I was a kid. When I met Natalie, it was usually on, but I wasn't paying attention. Then there was college, work, and well, life. I didn't even find as much time for reading.

And now, I didn't want to read. That was our thing to do together. Even books made me sad. Would I ever enjoy anything again?

I heard Grant in the kitchen, then watched as he walked into the hallway carrying a bottle.

What a pathetic pair we made. Both drinking our lives away. Though I had no idea why he was doing it with his. What a waste.

"Okay, pot, meet kettle."

Why was her voice so fucking active in my head? Why was I torturing myself?

After I heard Grant's bedroom door shut, I picked up the remote and flipped through Netflix.

We used Grant's friend's account and my neighbor's unsecure internet.

I glanced at the sad excuse for a dinner in front of me, and pushed it away before shifting back on the couch.

Although I was no longer hard from my shower, I knew I was only one memory away from being so again. Maybe even a small breeze at that point.

I clicked on a movie. I didn't know why I had chosen that one, but the fact that it had subtitles kept me on it.

I wasn't interested in listening to the words people said to each other. The fun corny dialogue or the I love yous would only continue to tear me up inside.

No, I just wanted to see sex scenes like I was watching cable porn as a teenager.

I wanted to jerk off to something that didn't bring up sad thoughts or make it impossible to finish.

I fast forwarded until I saw kissing.

Slipping my hands into my boxers, the breeze had already done its job.

My eyes shut out of habit, but behind the lids was Natalie. So I forced them open and on to the TV. I had picked the right movie. No fade to black. They were showing it all.

I did however consider turning down the volume, but I didn't want to lose my momentum.

The sex scene wasn't going to be long enough. I hadn't needed porn since before Natalie. "Fuck," I said out loud, pulling my hand from my boxers.

I exhaled and grabbed the remote, turning off the TV. It was useless. The woman was a part of me. Who knew how long it would be until everything in my life wasn't drenched in the loss of her?

I laid on the couch and rolled onto my side, going into the night as I had started my day. Staring at the couch cushions, begging for sleep and nothingness. While the Jack couldn't help me jack off, it did help me get a little sleep each night.

"Well, I think that's it. I think your bucket list is complete," I said to Natalie, trying to sound happy with that sentiment.

She grabbed the sheet of paper from me.

"Nope, you missed one."

My brows furrowed. "I did?"

She grabbed a pen from the kitchen table and wrote something down before she handed it back to me.

"Fuck on the beach," I read. "Shit, have we not done that?" I joked.

She shook her head and smirked.

I sat there, looking like I was contemplating her idea. I already knew it was a yes. I was just deciding on which beach.

"We could maybe plan it for this weekend," she began when I didn't say anything. "I mean, if you want to."

I smiled mischievously and jumped out of the chair, grabbing her hand and then the keys off the table.

"We can't go now," she said as we walked right out the door without our shoes.

"Why not?"

"It's eleven thirty at night."

"You wanted to wait until noon on a Saturday?" I asked with a laugh.

"Well, no, but—"

We stopped in front of the car.

"Do you want to fuck on a beach?" I asked her.

"Yes," she all but squealed.

"Do you want to fuck me *on a beach?"*

"Baby, I want to fuck you right here," she replied.

I exhaled. "Don't tempt me."

She smiled, biting her bottom lip.

"Get in the car. We're going to the beach."

She nodded.

"What about a blanket?"

"There's one in the back."

The thirty-minute drive to the nearest beach was filled with anticipation as her hand rubbed my upper thigh.

When we got there, a few people were enjoying the view of the beautiful night sky. So we walked—or jogged—down a little ways until no one was in sight.

I did my best to lay the blanket out on the sand, but the breeze kept messing it up.

But Natalie didn't care. She grabbed my shirt from the bottom, pulling it over my head. I put my lips on hers, my tongue tasting the mint she had stolen from my center console on the way over.

She playfully pushed me onto the blanket and climbed on top of me, pulling her shirt off and tossing it into the wind. She unbuttoned, then unzipped, my jeans and pulled them down with my boxers, freeing me.

I felt her hand and then her mouth as she took me inside of her.

My hands gripped her hair as I tried to keep my moans low enough so that we weren't caught, but loud enough that she knew what she was doing to me.

"I wanna fuck you," I said between moans.

She released me from her mouth, but her hand kept its rhythmic motion while she used her other hand to unbutton her shorts. She moved closer to me so I could pull them, along with her underwear, down. She then shimmied them off the rest of the way.

"We're naked on a beach," she said, straddling me.

"Nuh-uh, someone's still wearing her bra."

She smiled, pulling her hand off of me, and unclasped it from the back.

"Better?"

I nodded, and grabbed her ass, pulling her onto me.

I slid inside of her, listening to her sharp inhale and then immediate moan into the air.

There was no way I was going to last long.

The slight chill in the air only heightened the heat of our moving bodies. And while I was trying to keep quiet, my beautiful wife had not gotten the memo.

But I would have given the woman a microphone if that was what she wanted.

Fucking on the beach. That was what she had asked for. Out of all the things the woman could have requested—fucking me made the cut.

As her body tensed up, and her nails clawed at my chest, I released into her. Her back arched and her moans drifted into the night sky.

My eyes opened. I had hoped to dream to get away from the memories for just one night. But instead they found me there.

On the bright side, the built-up frustration had been worked out. I exhaled as I walked to my office and grabbed a new pair of boxers.

After I changed, I walked back into the living room and reached for my phone. I watched as the time changed to midnight.

My chest tightened as the tears that had been at the back of my eyes pushed their way forward.

I hadn't even realized the month, let alone the day. I didn't realize it was already time.

Tossing my phone to the ground, I grabbed the Jack I had conveniently left for myself just a short time earlier and put it to my lips.

After I downed what I could in a single motion, I raised the glass in the air to no one. "To the love we had," I choked out, and then put the bottle to my lips once more. "Happy anniversary, babe."

Chapter Eleven
{Sunday, July 15th, 2018}

"Leo?" Grant asked from the other side of the closet door.

Hide and go seek was an easy game when it was against a five-year-old.

"Mommy, I can't find Leo," Grant said.

"He's around here somewhere, baby. Keep looking."

I heard his footsteps recede, so I made myself comfortable in the closet, up against a bag of clothes ready for donation.

I shut my eyes for what seemed like only a second.

"He's gone!" I heard Grant exclaim as I was jerked awake, the bag of clothes tipping over against the door.

I grabbed the knob and ran out towards Grant's cries.

"See, he's right here," Mom said as I reached them.

"I'm so sorry, buddy. I fell asleep in the closet," I explained as I wrapped my arms around him.

"You fell asleep?" he asked, using the back of his hand to wipe his tears.

"Yeah, I was in your closet."

"My closet?"

"You didn't look in your *closet?" Mom asked.*

He shook his head, giving a small laugh along with her.

"I thought you were gone," he said, relieved.

"You don't ever have to worry about that. I'm never going anywhere."

"Are you even listening to me?" Diane asked, snapping her fingers in front of my face.

"Good luck getting anything out of him," Grant said, walking into the room.

"Fuck off," I retorted. "Don't talk about me like I'm not here."

"But *are* you?" he asked, opening the fridge and pulling out the orange juice and vodka.

Diane stared at him and then glanced at her Apple watch. "It's nine a.m., Grant."

"Oh, shit," he said, stopping in his tracks. "Starting late this morning," then kept walking to the cupboard with the glasses.

"Jesus, the two of you are a real shit show."

"Thank you," Grant replied, but I didn't respond.

His smile faded when I said nothing.

"You could at least be a fun drunk like me."

"Fun?" I asked. "You get plastered in my guest bedroom alone. How is that fun?"

My words implied I was upset about it, but my tone reflected how I really felt—indifferent.

"I'm not always alone."

"Excuse me?" I asked, losing my indifference.

He shrugged and then poured his drink. "Sometimes, after you've passed out, I invite guests over."

I jumped to my feet. "You let people into my fucking house?"

He took a swig from the bottle before pouring the rest of it into the orange juice. "Cool it. It's only one at a time—but never the

208

same woman twice," he said proudly, returning the juice to the fridge.

"You're having *sex* in my house?"

"Someone should be. What a waste of a house."

I shifted toward him as Diane got to her feet and pressed her hand firmly against my chest. "Hey, I only have so many Get Out of Jail Free cards for you to use."

Grant's eyes met mine and then went to Diane's. "Jail? What's she talking about, big brother?" he asked, intrigued by the new development in the conversation.

"Nothing," I replied, giving her a look of my own.

She seemed remorseful for her line. Or at least that it was in front of him.

"It's cool. Nothing a quick Google search won't tell me," he continued as he pulled out his phone and walked towards the stairs, drink in hand.

"He's having sex in my house," I said to her as she dropped her hand.

"So, you've had sex in mine."

"That was different."

"Why, because you were married?"

"No, because—" I began, but honestly, I didn't know why. I didn't have an excuse. "Whatever. Hopefully he at least wears protection."

"Well, that's a conversation for your department, not mine," she said with a laugh.

"What were you talking about before?" I interjected, not wanting to take part in whatever hilarity she found in our conversation.

Her mood swung like a pendulum. I was great at doing that to people. I didn't care that they were trying.

"Did you hear any of what I said?" she asked.

I shook my head. I should've been embarrassed by that.

"Well," she said with a sigh. "In summation, you're not getting any more life insurance money."

"Is this news?"

"I mean, it was to me. I've been trying to get it worked out for a while now."

"Sounds like a lot of wasted effort on your part."

She shook her head. "Clearly," she replied sharply as she grabbed her purse from the table and walked towards the door.

I should've gone after her. Apologized. But that wasn't me anymore.

The front door slammed shut, leaving me to be miserable to only myself.

***

"Damn, that's some mugshot," Grant said later that night as he walked into the living room where I had resided since Diane had stormed out.

"Fuck off," I retorted.

"Be nice or I'll send this to Mom."

I shot him a look.

"I really think the blood on your face brings out your eyes," he joked. "I'm just trying to figure out if that's yours or the other guy's."

"Seriously, Grant, I'm not in the mood."

"No? Oh, I'm sorry. Can you tell me when you will be, so I can come and banter with you then?"

I rolled away from him and faced the back of the couch.

"So, what'd this guy do to make you get a black mark on your clean record?"

"None of your fucking business."

"It's cool. I'll just Google that too," he replied with a chuckle. "The internet is such a wonderful thing—"

I jumped up from the couch, taking him by surprise. I ripped the phone from his hand and chucked it at the wall. It's possible the wall took the brunt of the damage.

"Are you fucking crazy?" he exclaimed.

"Maybe. Will you fuck off now like I asked?"

"God, my brother really isn't in there anymore, is he?"

"No, he's not. Now get the fuck out of the living room before I kick you the fuck out of my house."

I walked back over to the couch and repositioned myself to face the back of the couch as his footsteps headed back up the stairs.

"Stop it!" Grant yelled as he shoved a kid away from him.

"Aw, is little bitch gonna cry?" the boy asked Grant.

"Who you calling a little bitch?" I bellowed, taking them both by surprise.

I didn't give the kid time to respond. I grabbed a fistful of his shirt and brought him face to face with me.

"I don't know if you heard me," I said to him. "I asked who you were calling a little bitch."

"No one—" he replied with terror in his eyes.

"No one? It didn't sound like no one to me."

"I—I was saying it to Grant, but only because the other kids said it first."

"Other kids?" I asked.

"The kids at school. He cried in gym class and the other boys said it."

"I cry in gym class. Are you going to call me a little bitch?" I asked.

"Nnn—o," he barely managed to answer.

"If I find out that you, or any of those little fuckers, are talking shit about my brother again, I'll find you all and make you cry too."

He nodded, side-eyeing Grant.

"Now, what do you say to him?" I asked, tightening my grip on his shirt.

"Sorry."

"Great," I exclaimed, dropping him from my grasp. "Good chat."

The kid gave Grant one last look and took off running.

"He's going to tell his mom," Grant said, picking up his backpack and dusting it off.

"Yeah," I replied with a shrug. "I would love to be a part of that conversation when his mom calls ours. Mom will eat that woman alive."

Grant laughed, but it wasn't as full of life as it normally was.

"You okay?" I asked.

He nodded but was clearly lying.

"There's nothing wrong with crying," I said, putting my arm around his shoulder.

"No? Even in front of Melody?"

Grant was in the midst of his first real crush. I just hoped it worked out better for him than it had for me. But it didn't seem to be heading that way.

"If Melody doesn't like someone who shows emotions, then she's not worth it anyway."

"Big talk from a guy who doesn't have a girlfriend."

"Yeah," I replied with a chuckle. "Well, I'm just waiting for the right girl."

"One that you can cry in front of?" he asked.

"Exactly," I replied. "And, hey, I'm only sixteen, I've got plenty of time to find her."

I was startled awake by a pounding on my door. I jumped to my feet, forgetting for a minute where and when I was.

I rushed to the front door, seeing Mark through the glass.

"Leo," he said.

And even though it was just one word, I could tell he was drunk.

"What the fuck is going on?" Grant asked, walking halfway down the steps.

"Nothing. Go back to sleep."

"Is that Mark?" he asked.

"No. Now go back to sleep."

I didn't look at him, but my tone meant business. But when hadn't it lately?

I heard Grant walk back up the stairs, and I waited until his door shut before I opened the front door.

"Leo!" Mark exclaimed and then tried to walk in, but I didn't budge, so all he did was run into me.

"Listen," he said, taking a step back. "We need to talk," he continued, his eyes shining and his breath smelling like Jack.

"I said everything I needed to," I retorted as I took the edge of the door in my hand and attempted to shut it in his face.

He put out his hand and stopped it. "I didn't get to," he replied bitterly.

I pulled back on the door, searing my eyes into his. "Why do you think that is, Mark? Why do you *possibly* think I wouldn't let you explain?"

"I fucked up, I know—"

"—You know? You say it like you forgot to buy me a present for my birthday or dented my fucking car."

"It was a colossal fuck-up, I get that, but I'm paying for it now. Beth left me."

"Good. You fucking lied to her too."

"I know, and I thought that at some point I would love her like I—"

"—Like you loved Natalie?" I asked, my voice rising with my blood pressure.

"Yeah, see, you get it," he said, slapping his hand against my chest in a gesture of camaraderie.

Just how fucking drunk was he?

"No, I don't get it. How do you fall in love with someone else's wife?"

"Well, you weren't married when we met."

"Are you looking to get thrown up against the wall again?"

He exhaled. "I just mean, high school relationships don't last. I thought you two would break up."

"So what? You were biding your time?"

The blood rushed to my face as my hands clenched into fists.

"No—I mean—kinda. But I wouldn't have done anything without your permission."

My arms extended in front of me, shoving him onto the ground.

"This isn't coming out right," he said, staying down on the cement.

"No? Then what are you trying to say, Mark? Because what it sounds like you're telling me is we were only friends because you wanted to sleep with my wife."

"No," he exclaimed and did his best to quickly get to his feet. "No. You're my best friend. That's why I got with Beth after you guys got engaged, I gave up on any thought of her."

"That's a fucking lie, or we wouldn't be here right now."

He paused, and then nodded. "Okay, true. I had a moment of weakness and I kissed her." I stepped towards him, and he put up his hands and continued. "And it was stupid, and fucked up, and you deserved better."

"No, *she* deserved better. She didn't tell me that it happened. She never told me that you kissed her and said you loved her." He didn't know how to respond, so I continued. "You made her keep something from me, Mark. You made her go to the grave with a secret because she didn't want *me* to hurt. Because she didn't want *me* to kill you."

He nodded. "I'm sorry, Leo. I really fucked everything up."

"Yeah, you did."

"Do you ever think we could be friends again?"

"Maybe," I said, him looking up at me with hope. "If I were a bigger person," I continued. "But I'm not. So get the fuck off my property before I call the cops."

"Leo—"

I walked back inside and slammed the door behind me, trying to calm my rising heart rate.

The engine roared, then his tires squealed as he pulled away. I should've taken his keys. I should've had Grant drive him home.

I shut my eyes, leaning up against the door.

I heard the light click on as I opened my eyes and glanced at Grant at the top of the stairs.

"You, ah—got a little something," he said, wiping under his nose.

I pushed my fingers underneath, seeing red as I pulled them away.

"Yeah, happens sometimes," I responded as I walked towards the bathroom.

I heard his footsteps in quick succession down the stairs.

"What was that whole thing?" he asked, following behind me.

"None of your business."

"Mark loved Natalie?"

I rolled my eyes, keeping my nose pinched to try and slow the bleeding.

"He kissed her?"

"What about my demeanor says I want to be having this conversation?"

"I get it, but you need to talk about it with someone."

"Do I?" I asked, reaching the bathroom door.

"Yeah, you can't keep all of this in."

I spun around to face him.

"Why are you suddenly wanting to talk to me? You just took off when Nat died. You didn't even bother coming to her fucking funeral. You've been MIA since. So why now, Grant? Why do you give a fuck *now*?"

"Give a fuck? I've always given a fuck."

"You have a funny way of showing it," I said, grabbing the door to shut it.

He pushed his hand into it as Mark had to the front door. "Hey, you're not the only one who was fucking grieving."

"Don't give me that," I said, shaking my head.

"What? You're the only one who's allowed to miss her?"

"No, but don't act like it was some great tragedy so you can garner some fucking sympathy."

"Leo, you lost a wife, but I lost my sister. I've known her for the same amount of time as you."

The trembling of his voice brought me back to seeing my brother as a little boy. His scared, hurt tone said he wasn't just saying these things for a sympathy vote. He felt them.

"I didn't think—"

"—No, you didn't think—" I interjected.

"Grant, I'm sorry—"

He shook his head. "I don't need your apologies. I need my brother back."

I paused, turning my head to look at myself briefly in the bathroom mirror. I was again covered in blood, looking like the shell of the man I used to be.

"I'm sorry," I began again, looking his way. "But I don't think he's in there anymore."

Grant turned on his heels and walked away. He was still my kid brother. His stomping up the steps and slamming of his door told me that. But was I still *his* big brother? Would I ever again be the man he looked up to?

I shut the door to the bathroom and splashed water on my face, the sink turning pink.

I dabbed a towel against my face and then leaned on the counter, exhaling as I hung my head.

Grabbing a large bag out of the closet, I opened my drawer and threw some clothes into it.

"Why are you packing?" Grant asked from across the room.

"Teresa is taking me and Nat to check out University of Oregon tomorrow."

"And you need clothes for it?"

"We're staying the night."

"At the college?"

"No, at a hotel."

He shot up in his bed. "And Mom's letting you?"

I laughed and nodded. "I mean Teresa's going to be there too."

"Still—" he said, leaning back.

"Are you excited to have this room all to yourself next year?" I asked, glancing his way.

He shrugged but said nothing.

"Oh, come on. There's no way you aren't dying to get me out of here."

"Why would I want that?" he asked.

"I don't know," I replied with a shrug. "Just to have your own space."

"Why do I need my own space?"

"Because you're a twelve-year-old boy. Wouldn't it be nice to not have to take a shower every time you want to jerk off?"

He laughed. "Is that why you take so many showers?"

I threw the shirt that was in my hand at him. "Shut up. I don't take that many."

"Whatever. I heard Mom complaining about the water bill to Dad just yesterday."

"Yeah, well, I guess she'll be happy when I'm off to college too."

His smile faded.

"We won't see each other anymore after you go."

"What? Of course we will," I replied, walking over to him and grabbing my shirt from his bed. "It's less than two hours away. I'll be home on the weekends and holidays."

"You say that, but you'll want to be with Natalie."

"Well, yeah, but she can come too."

"You'll make friends."

"So?"

"You'll want to see them on the weekends to party."

My brows furrowed. "I mean, I do that now. What's the difference?"

"We share a room," he said. "You might always be busy, but at least you always come home."

I set down the clothes in my hand and glanced at my brother, who wasn't even looking my way. It hadn't even crossed my mind that he would be sad I was leaving. I was so excited to be free of rules, be free to be with Natalie at my own place, that I hadn't considered his feelings.

I walked over to his bed and sat next to him.

"Hey," I said softly. "I might not be home every night, but no matter where I am, I will always be your brother."

*** *

It had been days since Grant and I had talked to each other. Well, not just talked, but seen each other too. He was holed up in his room, coming out occasionally to use the bathroom, as I would hear the toilet flush. But he was back to being in his wing and I was in mine.

My guess was that he would come down and get food when I was napping. Maybe he was scaling the side of the house and going to the store to avoid running into me.

I walked into the kitchen and opened the fridge, finding the gruesome sight of an empty shelf where alcohol had once been.

I shut the door and glanced around the kitchen. Things to pawn were scarce in each room. I knew, especially after Diane's news the day before, that I was going to have to either go back to work soon or sell the house. But Wayne told me I couldn't come back until I was sober and less of an ass. Neither had yet to happen.

Guess I would be selling my house.

I grabbed my computer monitor from my office and walked to the front door.

I heard a door shut at the top of the stairs.

Maybe I should check on him.

"Maybe you should talk to him."

I exhaled, knowing I wasn't ready for that, but not knowing if I ever would be.

I set the monitor on the ground and walked up the stairs, standing in front of his closed door.

I knocked. Not wanting him to let me in just as much as I wanted him to.

The door opened. "Need the keys again?" he asked.

"No, uh, I'm making a liquor run." The pawn shop and liquor store were within walking distance, which was good, because I was in no condition to drive from the night before. "Any requests?"

His brows furrowed. He was used to drinking whatever I brought home.

"No, alcohol's alcohol at this point."

I nodded. "Okay," I replied, and began to shut his door, but then I stopped. "Grant," I began again.

"Hmm?"

"Why weren't you at Nat's funeral?"

His eyes dropped from mine. He swallowed. "It was too hard."

"You don't think it was for the rest of us?"

He nodded. "I knew it was. But I couldn't go."

"But why? I could've used my brother with me."

That hit him hard. It hit me hard too.

"I couldn't look at you," he said.

"Why not?"

He shook his head. "It doesn't matter."

"It does to me."

"Well, just because you want to know doesn't mean I have to tell you. I fucked up. It's done now."

Seemed there was a lot of that going around.

Grant got to his feet and started to walk past me. I grabbed his arm.

"Where are you going?" I asked, but not harshly.

"To see a man about a horse," he retorted, throwing my joke back at me.

"Are we just going to keep doing this?"

"Doing what, Leo?" he asked, pulling his arm from my grasp.

"Being assholes to each other."

"I'm only following in my big brother's footsteps—no wait, I'm sorry, he's not in there anymore." He walked out of the room and down the steps, that time with me chasing him.

"You haven't been the same since Nat got sick," I said to him.

"Well, you haven't been the same since you met her," he quipped, opening the front door and walking out.

"You're mad because I got a girlfriend fifteen years ago?"

"No, I'm just saying, if we are going to throw the past in each other's faces, we at least need to make sure it's all out there."

"I was seventeen."

"And I was twelve," he replied, whipping around to face me in front of his car.

"So?"

"So? My best friend disappeared overnight."

"What are you talking about?"

"The moment you met her, nobody else mattered to you."

"That's bullshit."

"Is it? Things have never been the same, Leo. And I get it, you loved her. I get why. She was an amazing woman. But she's dead now!"

"I know she is. What does that have to do with anything?"

"Because you're acting like you died too!"

I paused for a moment to assess his words.

"I did," I said softly.

"No, you didn't," he replied, walking over to me. "You were a whole ass human before you met her. You had a family, friends, people who loved you. And *we* are *still* here."

The agony in his voice brought tears to my eyes, but I was trying like hell to hold them in.

"The guy you were when you were with her might have died, but my brother didn't. He's still in there. I know it."

"If you're so sure of that, then why have you been pushing me away? Why weren't you around when I needed you?"

"Because I was preparing myself, Leo!" he exclaimed, and then looked to regret his outburst.

"Preparing yourself?" I asked. "Preparing yourself for what?"

"To lose you too."

Tears fell from his eyes.

And I again saw my little brother.

He was scared. Hurt. Tormented. And I did that to him.

He knew I didn't want to live without Natalie. He knew I didn't know how to function without my other half. He was trying to prepare himself to find my body one morning after I had finally given up and given in.

I guess I had been preparing everyone too.

I was distancing myself from everyone enough to where they would feel relief when I was gone instead of the grief I was in.

But they were all making it so hard. They all just kept holding on.

I walked over to Grant. He looked nervous, like I might hit him for what he said. And only being half sober, I understood the worry.

But instead of anger, I wrapped my arms tightly around him and held him close. His arms gripped me just as tight as he cried into my shoulder.

I had taught him that it was okay to cry. That it was okay to show emotion. To say fuck you to any person who told him otherwise. But there I was, still holding back, not wanting to feel any more pain than I already had been.

The few tears that had welled up in my eyes during the argument fell, but I held off on the others, wanting to comfort him, but wanting no part in being comforted.

After a few minutes, I released him from my grip, and he released me from his.

"The man I assaulted was Natalie's dad," I said.

I didn't know why I was telling him. Maybe I had been dying to tell someone.

"Holy shit," he said, using his entire hand to wipe the tears from his eyes. "Well, that explains a lot."

I nodded. "He tried to drop the charges once he learned who I was. But between the witness and him being in the hospital, the prosecutors decided to move forward anyway."

"Diane couldn't do anything about it?"

"She got it dropped down to a simple assault from an aggravated one."

"She's a good person to have on your side."

"Yeah, she is."

"You say that, yet you caused her to storm out of the house last time she was here."

"Yeah, I have a knack for making people do that," I replied with a smirk.

"Why was she so upset?"

I shook my head. "It's nothing. She's just looking into something for me," I said as we both walked back into the house.

I don't think he believed me, but he moved past it. Which I was grateful for, because I didn't have the heart to tell him we would both be back in Mom's house before the year was up.

Natalie sat next to me on the couch holding a cookie in her hand.

"I'm nervous."

"Nervous?" I asked with a chuckle.

"I haven't been high since I was in college."

I laughed. "I mean, just eat it slowly and you should be good."

She nodded, but then just stared at the cookie. "Will you eat some too?" she asked, turning towards me.

"You want me to be stoned too?"

"It will be fun!" she exclaimed with a smirk.

"This is supposed to be medicine for you."

"Russel said it's supposed to help with anxiety too."

I raised my brow. "Are you saying I have anxiety?"

She playfully nudged my side. "Oh, I'm sorry. Was it a secret?"

"I just thought I was hiding it better."

She shook her head. "Baby, you're starting to go gray."

My brows furrowed. "I found one white hair."

"That's how it starts."

"Whatever. I'll be a silver fox."

She repositioned herself to straddle me. "You most certainly will be."

The glimpse into the future made me sad. She saw that.

"Eat," she said, bringing it to my lips.

I opened my mouth and took a bite. "Okay, now you."

She followed suit.

I hoped with everything in me that the edibles brought her some relief. Her headaches had been getting worse. She was nauseous all the time, and she was barely eating.

But she didn't want the pain meds they were offering her. She didn't want to be knocked out for the remainder of her time with me. Selfishly, I didn't want her to be either.

So if the pot cookies, brownies and candy worked, I would have a little more time with my wife free of pain.

"We should call Grant," she said as she took another bite and then placed it back in front of my mouth so I could do the same. "I bet he would be fun to be high with."

I laughed. "I don't know if I could get high with my brother. Shouldn't I be setting a good example?"

"Oh, I'm sorry. Am I no longer a good example because I'm getting high?" she asked, raising her brows.

I poked at her side. "You're getting high because you're sick."

"Yeah, and everyone has an ailment that pot can help with."

"I didn't realize you were suddenly an expert."

"I talked to Russel about it for a while. I didn't realize how much it helps people. It just makes me think of all the times I spent feeling miserable from Lydia when I could have just smoked a joint."

I gave a small smile. "I'm sorry we didn't figure it out sooner."

"It's okay, lesson learned," she said, setting the cookie down on the side table and wrapping her arms around me. "And maybe it really will help calm you down a little bit."

"Calm me down? I am calm," I retorted.

"I just mean, mellow you out a little," she replied with a giggle. "I know how you are. You keep a lot of stuff inside. You're trying so hard to be strong for me—for everyone—but baby, at some point, you're going to have to let someone be strong for you."

Chapter Twelve
{Saturday, August 18th, 2018}

"I'll think about it," Grant said into the phone as I walked up the stairs to his room. "Yeah, I know. I know. I will—okay, bye."

"Who was that?" I asked, startling him from his doorway.

"Just a friend from college."

"What are you thinking about?"

"Why my brother is being creepy and listening to my phone conversations."

I shrugged and took the hint to move on. "I'm going to see Nat. I just wanted to let you know."

"Is that an odd way of telling me you're going to off yourself?"

I rolled my eyes. I knew his humor was the way he dealt with things. And I couldn't say he didn't learn it from me.

"No, I'm going to her grave," I replied.

His brows shifted up. "Oh, shit. Have you been yet?"

"No," I replied, shaking my head. "But I figured I'm as sober as I'm going to be, for a while anyway, so I might as well."

"Ya know, you could just get sober."

I pressed my lips together in a firm line. "Baby steps, brother."

He nodded.

"Well, I'll be here if you need me."

"Noted," I said, as I tapped the door frame and walked back out.

***

When I got to the cemetery, I pulled the blanket from the back seat and walked along the small trail to her headstone that lay beautifully against the green grass.

A small assortment of flowers rested at the top of the stone. Somebody had been there recently to visit. Someone clearly more thoughtful than her own husband.

Natalie's was the last one in the row. It made me feel better about sitting by her and not sitting on top of someone else.

I held on to the edge of the blanket and let the rest of it float into the air. Sand from our last trip to the beach blew into my eye.

"Fuck," I said, letting go of the blanket and rubbing away the grains in my retina.

Once I had successfully blinked it out, I fixed the blanket and took a seat on top of it. I could feel the remnants of the sand still burrowed in the fabric.

It reminded me of sex on the beach. It reminded me of a flat tire on the way home. Of sex in the back of the car after she watched me change the spare. It reminded me of her. Always of her.

My chest seized at the fact that I was lying next to my wife, but now it was with her six feet in the ground. I lay back on the blanket and swallowed a lump. Maybe I had come too soon.

Some would say I was months late.

"Everyone grieves in their own time."

I nodded to Natalie's words, closed my eyes, and let the sun warm my skin.

The phone rang from the kitchen as I sat at the dinner table with my parents and Grant.

"Can I get that?" I asked.

"No, we're in the middle of dinner."

"Yeah, but it might be Natalie."

"She knows what time we have dinner. She can wait until you're done."

The phone stopped ringing as I shoveled the cheesy potatoes into my mouth.

"Jesus, Leo, you're going to choke," my mom said.

"It's half an hour of your day, Leo. Just let us have this," my dad said.

I sighed and slowed my pace.

The phone rang again.

"Don't other people's children eat in this town?" my mom asked but stayed planted in her seat.

"Maybe it's important," I replied. "Maybe it's one of your clients, Dad."

He looked at me, knowing what I was doing. "Well, then, they'll have to wait for me to finish eating."

I exhaled and took a bite of my steak.

"We have an answering machine for a reason. You would think people would use it in this day and age," my mom commented.

"Maybe it's just a telemarketer. I've gotten a few of those calls now," my dad replied.

"But at dinner time? I mean, jeez, don't they have a family to eat with?"

The phone rang again.

"Oh, for Pete's sake," *my mom bellowed as she stood up.*

I now hoped it wasn't Natalie so she wasn't on the other end of my mom's temper.

"What is it?" *she asked in a stern voice as she picked up the phone.*

I expected her tone to grow firmer quickly after, but it didn't.

"What?" *she asked, her tone shifting.*

She disappeared out of the doorway where the dining room and kitchen met.

"How bad?" *I heard her ask, as I strained to listen over Grant's obnoxious chewing.*

She either walked further away or quieted down so that I couldn't hear her at all.

I stood up.

"Sit down, Leo," *my dad said, glancing up at me from his plate.*

"Something's going on," *I replied.*

"Okay, well, we'll find out what it is when your mom comes back in."

"What if—"

"Sit," *he demanded.*

"Leo," *my mom said. I hadn't even realized she had reentered the room.* "Okay, I don't want you to freak out," *she began.*

"What is it Rita?" *my dad asked, his tone shifting too.*

She didn't take her eyes off me. "There's been an accident—"

"—Who?" I asked.

But the look on her face told me before her words did.

I bolted past her to the front door.

"Leo, give me your keys," my mom shouted after me.

"No, I need to see her."

"Leo, you can't drive like this."

"What did they say? What happened?" I asked, continuing to walk to my car.

"Teresa was on her way to the hospital herself. She didn't have any news yet."

I opened my car.

"Leo, stop," my mom pleaded.

"Leo," my dad snapped, walking quickly to me and grabbing me out of the car. "Your mother said you can't drive."

"I need to see her," I exclaimed, the panic rising in my voice.

He nodded. "Then I'll drive you." He took my place in the driver's seat as I ran to the passenger side.

The sound of the grass being cut forced my eyes open. The hum was actually calming. It had been a while since I had been outside and heard that noise. It reminded me of summers spent in my backyard as a kid. When dad would mow the grass and I would lie on the patio soaking in the sun, reading a book. The summers before my life was consumed by Natalie.

It was a time that was so distant now and filled with a person that was unrecognizable to me.

233

I took a deep breath, readjusting myself to my memory. It had been the scariest day of my life as a teenager.

I thought Natalie had died that day. The whole way to the hospital I was sick to my stomach. Literally. My dad had to pull over so I could vomit on the side of the road.

Exhaling, I rolled onto my side and faced Natalie's headstone that lay like a concrete pillow next to me.

"I was only seventeen when I thought I lost you," I began. "I had only known you for eleven months when I got that call, but it was like my world was on the edge of imploding at the news of you being gone."

A small bug walked across her name. I moved my hand to squash it, but then stopped.

There was enough death in that place.

"I should've known then I was in over my head. That I loved you too much. I was a kid, Nat. We were just kids. How was it possible I knew then that I couldn't live without you?"

A tear dripped onto the blanket, soaking right into the fabric.

I rolled on to my back once more and stared up at the sky.

How was it possible that the world still turned? That the sun still rose? That the grass still needed to be cut? That people's lives just continued on?

"It doesn't make sense," I began again. "If there is a God, why did he save you that day, but not this time? Why would he give us years to build a life together, just to rip them away?"

The tears fell down the side of my face, pooling uncomfortably into my ears.

"Why leave you here to experience pain? To experience loss? Why not take you before life got too hard, and too complicated? Before Lydia. Before Glen. Before the miscarriages. Why would anyone put one person through all of that?"

"Because I got to be with you."

I shut my eyes at the sound of her voice.

"What a shitty deal," I choked out with a chuckle. "You had to go through all of that, and all you got was me in return."

I took a deep breath and wiped my face. All I could hear was my brother saying Sad Sack Leo, or Mr. Pity Party. But he wasn't wrong.

That's all I was. Even without an audience.

"Next week, man," Mark said, slapping my shoulder. "One more week and you're officially a married man."

I nodded and smiled.

"I wish you would've let us plan something a little more elaborate for your bachelor party," he continued.

"We're twenty," I replied. "How elaborate do you think we could get on our budget?"

He laughed. "Something a little better than drinking in a friend's basement."

"We aren't old enough for bars."

"I could have gotten us fake IDs."

"Yeah, but no one would believe Grant's 21," I said, glancing over at him.

He laughed. "Well, your brother didn't have to come."

"Of course he did. He's my brother."

"Whatever. Still, booze aside, we could have gotten strippers or something."

"This is my bachelor party, not yours."

"True enough," he replied with a laugh. "I want Vegas for mine."

"Well, I guess your best man will have lots of planning to do."

"Shut up, prick. You know that shit's going to be on you."

"If I accept."

"You will."

"You gotta actually commit to a woman for that to happen."

"Joke's on you because things are starting to get serious with Beth."

"What? No way."

"Why is that so hard to believe?"

"Because you just met."

He rolled his eyes. "Oh, I'm sorry. is love at first sight only saved for you and Nat?"

I playfully pushed his shoulder. "Shut up. If you really are, then I'm happy for you, man. Nat will be too. She thinks Beth's good for you."

"She said that?"

"Yeah, I know she doesn't always show it, but she thinks you're a good guy. She just wants you to be happy."

He smiled, his eyes growing softer than I'd ever seen them.

"That's really nice to hear," he said, nodding his head. "That's a good woman you got there."

I smiled, putting the cup to my lips to finish off my drink. "The best."

A grinding sound filled the air, causing me to lift my head. I squinted, my eyes adjusting to the sun overhead.

The man on the mower turned it off and stepped down to the ground, letting out a few choice words in the process.

I watched as he kicked it and then ran a handkerchief over his receded hairline.

I got to my feet and walked over to him. When I was about ten feet away, he noticed me.

"I'm sorry," he said, looking remorseful. "I didn't mean to disturb your visit."

"It's okay. What happened?" I asked, nodding to his mower.

"I think some wiring from the fence got caught in it. I'm sure it's an easy fix, but my hands just aren't as steady as they used to be. That's why I took this job. Sitting on the mower a few times a month ain't too bad of a gig."

I nodded. "Mind if I take a look?"

He shrugged. "Be my guest."

I got down on my hands and knees and looked underneath it.

"Yeah, I see some wire—"

"—Shit," he replied.

I stood back up and wiped my hands together to remove the loose grass. "Do you have a screwdriver?"

"Ah, yeah," he replied. "Over in the shed."

"Okay, I should be able to grab the wiring out. I had one of these when I interned back in college for a landscaping company. I'm sure the set-up hasn't changed too much."

He nodded and walked over to the shed, disappearing behind the door, and then coming out with what I needed.

"I wasn't sure which type you would need so I grabbed the interchangeable one."

"Perfect," I said, taking it from his hand.

I knelt back down on the ground and took out the battery and spark plugs. Once everything was removed, I tugged on the wire until it was free. Then I put everything back in its place.

"I really appreciate the help," he said as I handed the screwdriver back to him.

"No problem," I said, wiping my hands on my jeans.

I wasn't sure what the etiquette was anymore for small talk. But I had served my purpose there, and he either sucked at small talk also, or felt I had served my purpose as well.

I walked back over to Natalie, and lay back down on the blanket, resting my arm under my head.

It was getting entirely too hot out for the jeans I was in, but that was the most time I had spent outside since the across town jog I had done months before.

I closed my eyes, letting the light breeze cool me down.

"Okay, so I don't know if this is really morbid or really sweet," Diane said at the front of a private room in Natalie's favorite restaurant. *"But Nat came to me and said she wanted a funeral, and I was like, duh, we had planned on it. And then she said, 'No, before I die.'"* Diane sighed. *"And, I mean, what do you say to your dying best friend?"*

Diane choked on the words, but she passed it off through a chuckle.

I don't think Natalie noticed, but it was probably because I had tensed up at the words as well, so she had started rubbing my leg to calm me down.

"So, as the overachiever that I strive to be, I went to task with talking to and inviting everyone to a funeral for a person who was still alive."

Everyone laughed.

"It was awkward, okay—I was awkward. But either way, they all agreed." She exhaled. *"But then someone said to me, that they would go, but that they wouldn't talk. And I was like, well that's hella' rude,"* she continued, narrowing her eyes. *"But then she explained that she would just cry and that she didn't want to cry in front of Nat. And believe me, I understood."*

Natalie tilted her head at Diane's words. Diane returned the sentiment.

"But I guess Nat had the same worry, because she decided she didn't want to do that anymore, and again, how do you say no to your dying best friend?"

I'd like to say she said it easier that time, but it still hit. Nat saw, and I watched her swallow back a sob.

I squeezed her hand.

"So, since I had gone to all that trouble," she mocked, but then winked at Natalie. "I decided to video their words for you instead."

Natalie put her hand to her chest as a tear ran down her cheek.

"I put six boxes of tissues on the table. That's how many I went through putting all this together, so you may need more, I don't know. Luckily for you, I edited out all the people that said you were an evil bitch. So if you don't see Leo's in here, that's why."

We all laughed, as I shook my head at Diane, while Natalie laughed through the tears that were falling a little faster now.

I squeezed her hand again and then kissed her cheek. "If you need us to pause it, you just let us know," I whispered, before kissing her once more.

Diane turned off the light and plugged a small projector into her phone that was aimed at the beige wall.

She took a seat on the other side of Natalie and tipped her head onto her shoulder. "Happy Birthday, Bestie."

Nat kissed Diane's head and leaned onto it as the video began.

I don't know if it was the sun that was getting to me, or the fact that I was sober for the first time in months. But a wave of nausea ran through my body, and I was starting to ache from head to toe.

I exhaled. I didn't want to leave her yet, but I also knew I would have to at some point. I was more than likely dehydrated, and sitting in the California sun all day wasn't going to bode well.

I sat up, breathing through the salivation that comes right before the contents of my stomach.

I closed my eyes, trying to focus on something other than the feeling I was experiencing. Hoping I could ride the wave.

"Grant got offered a job," I said. "He doesn't know that I know, but I've overheard a few conversations now. So I pieced it together."

I ran my hand through my beard and kept it over my mouth for a second.

"It's in New York. I think that's why he hasn't told me," I paused. "I think he's scared to leave me."

The wave of nausea passed, and I opened my eyes, looking at her gravestone. "And honestly, I'm scared to let him."

I laid my head back down on the blanket, hating that Natalie couldn't talk back. But I knew her well enough to have both sides of the conversation.

As much as I wanted to be selfish and keep my brother around, I knew I couldn't ask that he put his life on hold for me.

He had spent the year grieving the loss of his sister. I finally understood that. It more than likely contributed to the blow-up of his company. He had been put through the wringer, and the fact that he was even entertaining the phone calls told me he was ready to come out the other side.

As long as I didn't stand in his way. As long as I didn't allow us to stay drunk all day every day. As long as he didn't think that was all I would do without him there with me. He needed to see hope.

That was going to be the hard part. Especially when I didn't see it myself.

"That was such a beautiful video," Natalie said on the way home from the restaurant.

"Yeah, she did a fantastic job."

"Do you really think people think all of those nice things? Or were they just saying them because I'm dying?"

I laughed. "I think, if it were anyone else, they would have just been saying it. But I know that everything they said was true about you."

She glanced lovingly at me. "You're biased."

I nodded. "Doesn't mean I'm wrong though."

She started to laugh, but it trailed off quickly.

"Are you okay?" I asked, my body tensing up.

The doctors had given her six months to a year. We had shattered the six-month timeline, but as the year approached, I was on edge knowing that any moment could be our last.

She shut her eyes and pressed her hand to her head.

The fucking headaches. The fucking pain she was in. I just wished I could take it all away.

"Do you have any of your edibles?"

She carefully shook her head.

"Okay, well, we'll be home soon. We can get stoned together."

I saw a small smile grow on her face.

I took a deep breath and focused on the road.

When we pulled into the driveway. I turned off the car and ran to the other side.

"I'm okay," she said, as I put my hand in hers to help her out. "I don't need your help," she continued softly as she kept her hand on her head.

"I know, just—"

"—Leo, I don't need your fucking help!" she yelled, shoving me away from her.

Fucking Glen. The prick wasn't only hurting her, but was making her angry, bitter. I didn't hold anything she said against her, but it was always still hard in the moment.

She slowly walked, her hand on her head, eyes barely open to watch where she was going.

I shut the car door and walked a few paces in front of her to unlock the door.

As I put my keys into the lock, I glanced back at her. She had stopped.

"Leo," she said, her tone soft once more.

Before I could answer, her eyes rolled into the back of her head.

I moved in one swift motion to her, catching her before she hit the ground.

Her body started to seize, so I rolled her on to her side and did my best to follow the instructions her doctor had lined out.

I hated that it was something I was getting better at. I hated that, every time she had one, I was scared she would wake up not being able to talk. Or walk. Or worse, that she wouldn't wake up at all.

When my eyes opened again, my heart was racing.

Another wave of nausea moved through.

Where were the edibles when I needed them?

I took a deep breath and slowly got to my feet, knowing my condition was only going to get worse in the California heat. "I'm sorry I can't stay longer. Maybe in the future, staying sober for visits won't be so hard."

I grabbed the blanket, then knelt down next to the stone. I put my hand to my lips and then pressed it to her name. "Happy Birthday, babe."

***

The hair of the dog that bit me worked like a charm. And while that was comforting to my insides, it was a terrifying realization of just how bad I had let things get with my drinking.

I wished I could say that that alone would change my behavior. But it wouldn't. Maybe if it wasn't Natalie's birthday. Maybe if I was still going to work. Maybe if it wasn't a Saturday. Or maybe if I didn't have to tell my brother to leave me and go live his life.

Maybe if all of those things weren't happening, I would have checked myself in and gotten help. But more than likely, I would've just been ready with other excuses.

Because really, I knew I wasn't ready to go back to our life. I wasn't ready to begin again in the world we had built together. I wasn't ready to move through it alone.

"How was Nat?" Grant asked, dropping his body weight full force into the chair across the living room from me.

"Quiet."

He smirked.

I did too.

"It was good weather today," he said, glancing at the bottle on the coffee table in front of me, but just as quickly looking away.

"Do you want some?" I asked, ignoring his odd comment about the outside world.

He shook his head. "I'm good."

I gave a side smile. "I haven't had to make as many liquor runs lately."

"That's good."

"Yeah," I said with a nod. "Weird though, because I haven't slowed down much."

He shrugged. "I just haven't felt like drinking the last couple of weeks."

"Does that have anything to do with the job offer?"

He repositioned himself in the chair. "Job offer?"

I raised my brow. "The one in New York."

"No idea what you're talking about."

Was he always that good of a liar? Had I not heard the conversation with my own ears, I would've believed him.

"So your college friend hasn't been trying to get you to come work for him in New York?"

"I think I would've told you if I had gotten offered a job."

"Yeah?"

"Of course. That's kind of big news."

"So, there's no way you would be offered a job and turn it down."

"Absolutely not."

His lying was actually starting to irritate me. But that may have been the whiskey.

"Okay, so if I were to call that Kenny guy back, he would say there's no job?"

"My God, you're worse than Mom," he replied, rolling his eyes. "There's no job in New York. There's no job offer period."

"So, why haven't you been drinking?"

"Maybe because someone needs to start being the responsible adult here."

"Why?" I asked, but it wasn't because I didn't agree. I was just hoping I could push his buttons until he confessed.

"Why?" he spat back. "Look at us. We're both unemployed, drinking a fifth each a day, and living off frozen Banquet meals."

"Michelina's," I corrected.

"Jesus, whatever," he said, getting to his feet. "Regardless, this shit can't go on forever."

"I agree," I said, as calmly as ever.

"You do?"

I nodded. "That's why you have to take the job."

"Jesus, Leo, there is no—"

"—Cut the shit, Grant," I interjected.

He exhaled, running his hand through his hair. "I'm not taking it," he finally said.

"Like hell you're not. I'm not letting you put your future on hold for me."

"Who says it's for you? Not everything's about you, Leo."

"If it's not about me, then why wouldn't you take it?"

"Because I'm scared."

I rolled my eyes. "Bullshit, Grant."

"I'm serious. It's a huge risk. Moving across the country, starting up a business with Kenny—"

"Since when does risk scare you?" I asked.

"Since I failed."

I shook my head. "I don't believe you."

"Why?"

"Because you are many things, little brother, but scared of risk isn't one of them."

"You don't know shit."

"No?" I asked, standing up and meeting his eyeline. "Grant, you've taken risks your entire life and, until last year, they always paid off. I know a little setback like that doesn't change who you are."

"Says the guy who did a complete one-eighty in one year."

"That's different."

"How?"

"You lost a business. I lost my wife."

"Yeah, but we both crashed and burned after."

"Yes, but you can recover. You can move on and start again."

"So can you!" he exclaimed with an exhale. "Stop acting like this is it. Like life is over."

"I know it's not. I know it will get better at some point. I'm just not ready for that yet."

"Well, maybe I'm not either."

"Because of me," I stated.

"Of course, because of you!" he exclaimed again, choking back a sob. "I'm scared, Leo. I'm fucking terrified. If I walk out that door, what does that mean for you? Who's here for you?"

"That's not your problem."

"Like hell it's not."

"Grant, I'm not your responsibility."

"And I'm not yours. You don't get to tell me to take a job if I don't want to. If you're hell-bent on wallowing in your misery, then I'm going to wallow too."

"No, you don't get to give up your future and have me to blame."

"But you get to give up on yours?"

"Grant, it's different," I replied as I shook my head and exhaled. "You have an opportunity to get out. Stop hanging on."

"Do you even hear yourself? Should I just record you on my phone and play it back? Would the pep talk work if it was coming from you?"

"Stop turning this around. Forget about me and my life for two fucking seconds. What do you want to do?"

"I want you to listen to yourself."

"No, not with me. What do you want for yourself!" I bellowed.

"I want to move to New York!" he shouted back, and then looked to regret it.

The room fell silent.

"Good, then it's settled. You'll call Kenny and take the job."

"Leo—"

"Take it or not, Grant. Either way, you're out of the house by the end of the month."

I wasn't sure if it was relief, anger, or sadness that crossed his face. More than likely, it was a mixture of all three. I think I had the same expression.

I was relieved I wasn't going to hold him back. I was angry that I had been. And I was sad that someone else was moving forward, and I was just sitting in place.

Grant left the room as I fell back onto the couch, worn out from the surge of emotions.

I grabbed the bottle and took a sip, listening as Grant made the phone call I had been praying he would make.

"Grant," I whispered, nudging him awake. "Grant," I said again.

"Leo? What is it?"

I smiled as I set some clothes on top of his blanket. "Get dressed and be quiet."

His brows furrowed.

"And I would pick up the pace a little or we'll be late."

That made him move faster.

It was my last night home before I left for college. All of my friends were at a party. I was going to be too. But when I was getting ready to leave, Grant started crying.

He had tried to hide it. He got angry and passed it off like he was pissed about something. He had locked me out of the bedroom. But we both knew full well that I knew how to break in.

"Ready," he whispered excitedly.

"Great! Follow me."

"Uh, do Mom and Dad know we're leaving?"

"If they did, would we be whispering?"

He smiled, following me out of the bedroom door.

They actually did know.

When he had locked me out, I went downstairs and talked to Mom. Grant had been moody for the past month. Honestly, I figured it was thirteen-year-old bullshit. I had gone through it too. But Mom said they had talked. She said she had promised not to say anything. But he was sad I was leaving. He was scared to be alone in his room. He was scared to be at school without me. He was scared I wouldn't come back.

How could I go to a party if my brother was hurting? If my brother was going to miss me?

We climbed into my car and put it in neutral as I guided it down the driveway.

"Is this how you've been sneaking out?" he asked, wide-eyed.

"Don't get any ideas, kid," I said as if I wasn't just five years older and just as stupid.

He smiled as I closed my door and started the engine once we were on the street.

"Don't you want to know where we're going?" I questioned, finding it odd he had yet to ask.

"I don't care where we go," he replied with a shrug. "I'm just excited to hang out with you."

Chapter Thirteen
{Sunday, September 23rd, 2018}

The doorbell rang. Then a knock on the door. Doorbell, knock, doorbell in quick succession, each knock louder than the one before.

"If you don't do something about this lawn, I'm calling the cops!"

I assumed that was my angry neighbor. Although I wasn't sure which one. They had all seemed to stop by in the last month. Although none were bringing baked goods like I had seen on TV.

"Just explain to them that I died."

Why? Shouldn't they assume that by the lack of her being around? Or at the very least that she left me? Either one would be grounds for depression, right?

Maybe we should've made more of an effort to get to know them over the six years we had lived there. To be fair, most of them were pretty new themselves. They wouldn't know to have even an inkling that something was wrong by my lawn being as unkempt as myself. They didn't know what I did for a living.

They didn't know my wife had died and the insurance agency was corrupt and fucked me out of the money I was owed. They didn't know I was too drunk to work. Though they probably wouldn't have cared about that last part.

They just knew the man at the end of the block had a nice ass house and no longer paid for the same lawn care service that they did.

When the pounding stopped, I walked into the kitchen and grabbed the last fifth of Jack.

Shit. I was going to have to go out.

But with what money?

What was left to pawn?

I looked at my wedding ring and immediately shut my eyes. I would rather die going cold turkey. Maybe that would happen.

I screwed off the cap and took a swig. The burn had worn off months before. Either I was numb to the feeling, or I had burned off the nerves in my throat.

When I walked back into the living room, my phone vibrated on the coffee table. I was surprised it still had a charge.

I only charged it once a week. The day I had to call my mom. It was enough to keep her in Oregon and prevent her from seeing me the way I was. It also kept Grant in New York. Though he said he would be back for Thanksgiving.

But that wasn't the threat he thought it was.

The phone stopped vibrating and I looked at the screen. Teresa.

Honestly, I thought my mother-in-law had forgotten I existed. I hadn't seen or talked to her since before Thanksgiving the previous year. Since before she went on vacation with her boyfriend.

Shit, I probably should have been concerned that she had died while away. Maybe she'd been mad that whole time.

Or maybe *I* should have been.

The phone vibrated again. Back to back calls. No voicemail.

Did something happen?

What? Like my wife dying? What bad news could she possibly have?

If I really believed she didn't have any, I would've picked it up. I wouldn't have been terrified to say hello and see how she was holding up. But I was, so I didn't. It stopped again.

Low battery flashed across the screen. Soon it wouldn't matter. It would be dead again. I would be shut off from the outside world once more.

"She's getting worse, Leo," Teresa said as I walked back to my bedroom with Natalie's water.

"She's fine," I lied. Both to her and to myself.

"That makes three seizures today."

"One less than yesterday."

"It's only noon."

I exhaled. "What do you want me to say, Teresa?"

She looked caught off guard by my tone. "I just want you to prepare yourself."

"What the hell do you think I've been doing for the last year?"

"Lying to yourself."

I shook my head, finding a few choice words. But she interjected before I could use them. "I just want you to understand what the doctors are saying. She already can't walk. Soon she won't be able to talk. Then she won't—"

"Jesus Christ, I get it. Now can I please just go be with my wife?"

She sighed, knowing I didn't get it. But there was nothing she could say to pull me out of my denial.

I had a couple weeks at most left with her, maybe even days, but that reality wasn't sinking into the emotional side of me. It was factual. I understood. But emotionally, I didn't. I couldn't.

I had fallen asleep. Maybe passed out. The two were one and the same now.

I flipped on the TV. The screen was blue. I was on the right input. Neighbors must have locked their Wi-Fi. Or Grant's friend finally changed his Netflix password. Maybe both.

I turned it back off as my phone entered its permanent slumber.

If my eyes were open, I wouldn't know if I couldn't feel them. Getting up to pee was going to be an ordeal. Pinky toes would most certainly be stubbed. I would probably knock over a box of photos.

My hand clung tight to the glass bottle. At least I didn't need to see to be able to drink. Not as long as I didn't put it down. And that was the plan. Hold on to it until it was gone. Or until I passed out again. Either one was acceptable.

I walked into our bedroom and sat on the bed next to Natalie.

"Gotcha some water," I said as she looked at me.

She smiled. Or did her best to anyway.

But I could see in her eyes she was happy I was back.

I hated every second I left the room. I did my best to do it as little as possible.

Twisting off the cap, I put a straw into it and put it to her lips.

"Thanks, baby," she whispered as she cleared her throat.

I nodded and set it on the nightstand.

"What do you want to watch?"

She smiled. "We haven't finished Grey's yet."

"Of course," I replied with a playful eyeroll. "How could I forget about Grey's?"

She smiled.

I turned on the TV and snuggled up next to her. She slowly moved her hand and intertwined her fingers with mine.

I looked at her as the episode began. She had lost a good amount of weight in the past month. She didn't react well to food. I joked and said it was because it was my cooking and not hers. But when my mom got in a few days earlier and started cooking, the joke didn't land as well.

"So which one's McDreamy again?" I asked.

She rolled her eyes. She knew I knew. I loved pushing her buttons.

"How many more seasons do we have?"

"Two," she replied. "Plus the newest season that hasn't been added yet."

"Damn. Three more?"

"Yeah, I don't think I'll make it."

She stared at the screen. So I turned and did too. She was acknowledging it better than I was. Or maybe she was just being factual without emotions too.

She sighed. I wasn't sure if it was her comment or if she was getting uncomfortable again. I was in charge of her pain medication. It was hard not to give it to her the second she was hurting. But she also wanted to be as lucid as possible.

"Want a cookie?"

She nodded. I opened the drawer on the nightstand and pulled out the Tupperware container. Once the lid was off, I put the cookie to her lips.

"You first," she said.

I laughed. "I'm good."

"Are you going to make me be stoned alone?"

I laughed again. "I can't believe I'm still being subjected to peer pressure at thirty-one."

"That's life, kid," she replied with a shrug.

I took a bite and then put it back to her lips. She did the same.

Fuck. I had to pee. Goddamn Jack. Goddamn lack of light. I stood up, and immediately stubbed my toe on the coffee table. "Fuck," I snarled.

I continued to stumble my way to the bathroom, hitting the kitchen light just before I finished my walk. That way I could see on the way back.

See, I was still lucid enough to think straight. But it was a bummer that I wasn't nearly as drunk as I would've hoped to be at that point in the night.

After flushing the toilet and avoiding the mirror all together, I walked back through the house to the living room. I let my body fall into the grooves that had been formed to fit my body on the couch cushions. My very own Leo shape. That in itself was depressing.

I took another swig from the bottle and then rested my head back. My eyes closed, Natalie's face appearing behind my eyelids. For a moment she was seventeen again. Then twenty. Then twenty-eight. And eventually thirty-two. The oldest she would ever be.

I opened my eyes, preferring that darkness to her light. Picturing her just made everything hurt. The memory of her. Of our final weeks together. Our final days. It was unbearable. It was agony.

"Wake up, sleepy head," I whispered to Natalie as her eyes opened.

I cleared my throat, hoping it would stop the trembling. She was awake. There was still time.

"I have a surprise for you."

"What is it?" she asked, her dry lips curling into a smile.

"You'll just have to see."

I grabbed her Burt's Bees Chapstick from the bedside and rubbed it on her lips before I walked to her side of the bed.

"Kiss me," she said. So I did.

"I'm going to pick you up, okay?"

I was nervous to do so. I was scared to hurt her. I was scared the cookie we had eaten only a few hours before had worn off and that every movement would be agony.

But if she was feeling any pain at all, she didn't show it.

I carried her slowly through the house.

My parents had left for the store, and Teresa was cooking for everyone with Diane.

I walked through the French doors onto our back patio. She shut her eyes and leaned her head back.

"Are you okay?" I asked nervously.

"Yes," she paused as a smile crossed her face. "I just missed the breeze."

I walked through our backyard as the sun prepared to set. The tiki torches I had placed in the ground guided my way.

The queen size mattress and box spring from the guest room lay on the grass. Blankets and pillows were made up perfectly, like it was ready for a house showing.

The tiki torches lit up the whole area as I laid her on one side of the bed.

"What is this?" she asked.

"It's a date."

"It's our first date," she said in a reminiscent tone.

I nodded. "With a little more padding."

She laughed, then coughed.

"And drugs. Just in case," I continued as I grabbed the Tupperware from the ground.

She smirked.

"Hungry?"

She nodded.

I grabbed a cookie and put it to her lips.

"You first."

"Do you think these are poison or something? I'm sorry, but I refuse to be your test subject every time," I joked.

She laughed, wincing as she did. That hurt me, because all I ever wanted to do was make her laugh.

"I refuse to be stoned alone," she said.

I grinned, acting like it was a big deal to take the first bite. "But if my reading's off, I'm blaming the cookie."

"You're going to read to me?" she asked, her tone as joyful as her eyes.

"Of course. You think I would just bring you outside to watch the sunset and star gaze?" I exhaled. "I'm much more romantic than that."

She nodded. "Guess you learned from the best."

"Guess so."

After she ate a few bites, I set the cookie back in the container and grabbed the book from the ground.

"My eyes are shut," she said, then paused while she took a few breaths. "But I'm not sleeping."

I smiled and kissed her forehead before I began. "It is a truth universally acknowledged that a single man in possession of a good fortune, must be in want of a wife."

I glanced over at her as she smiled once more.

"I love you," she said, looking more content than she had in weeks.

Tears sprang to my eyes and burned. I tried to hold them back. "I love you too," I replied as evenly-toned as I could.

She slowly shifted next to me. Using all the strength she had to put her arm around me and her head on my shoulder.

I kissed her head, cleared my throat, and continued on.

After a little while, she had fallen asleep and there was a chill in the air.

I shifted beside her as her eyes opened.

"Where are you going?" she asked.

"We should get back inside. It's getting cold."

"I'm not ready," she said with a sigh, knowing it might be her last time outside. "Two more minutes?"

I grinned and shifted my body next to hers once again. "Two more minutes."

***

The screech of the doorbell pierced my ears. Then the banging on the door again. I hadn't expected them so early. But the sun was up, and the yard was still in shambles.

I wished they would just call the cops already. Well, maybe not. Maybe just hold off for a few more hours. That's all I needed.

No, not hours. An hour?

I grabbed the bottle of whiskey, seeing I had just enough left. I had been worried I was going to have to make a trip to the store. Pawn one more thing. But I had been resourceful. Silver lining?

The neighbor had given up faster than usual. Good for them. It was a waste of time anyway. I wasn't going to answer.

I walked down the hall to my bedroom door. *Our* bedroom door. The room that we moved our stuff to years before when we needed a change—swapping our guestroom with the old master. That fore-thought came in handy in the last few months of her life.

I sighed, clenching the bottle in one hand, and using the other to turn the knob.

I don't know what I had expected when walking in there. Maybe for her to still be lying in the bed. The thought of the corpse made me sick. The thought of her dying there exactly one year before almost brought me to my knees.

I stepped through the threshold, glancing around at the dust that had settled on top of all her belongings. There were so many things in there to pawn. The thought of going in there hadn't even occurred to me. I don't think it would have changed anything. I hadn't been ready then.

Well, I wasn't ready at that moment either. But that was the only room that held what I needed. It was the only room that held any real comfort. Not because of the memories. No, her dying in there ruined that.

It held comfort because it held her pills. Her opioids. The prescription for her pain management, that was now going to be for mine.

Only I wasn't there for the managing part so much as taking it away.

I closed the door and walked to the nightstand that had a small tub on top that held six bottles. Each of which contained something different. I shook each one to see which held the most.

My legs shook underneath me and then gave way, causing me to sit on my bed. It moved against my weight. Everything slowed.

Except my heart.

Pushing down on the cap, I twisted and then pulled it off, opening my palm for the contents to fall into. A tear fell onto the little white pills, making them look glossy. I closed my eyes, feeling a few more tears stream down my face.

"Promise me you won't grieve for too long," she said, causing me to stop reading mid-sentence.

"What?" I asked.

Her eyes stayed shut. Either because she was too tired to open them, or because she didn't want to see my expression.

"I know it will be hard for you—" she began and then took another breath. "But I need you to promise me."

"I can't promise that," I said, resting the book on my chest.

Her eyes opened, using most of her strength. She fought me with what little she had left. "One year, Leo. That's all you get."

"One year?"

She nodded. "I want you to promise me you will grieve for one year and not a day longer."

"Nat—"

"No. Promise."

Her eyes were filled with tears. As dehydrated as she was, I still had been able to make her cry. I never wanted to make her cry.

I closed my eyes and put my forehead to hers. "Okay, babe. One year."

I picked the glass bottle back up from the nightstand, the pills trembling in my other hand.

"One year, babe," I said to Natalie. To the universe. To anyone that was listening. "I promised one year."

I put the handful of pills to my mouth, holding my chaser by the neck of the bottle.

"Leo!" Teresa exclaimed from the doorway.

I glanced up to see the door hit the wall and Teresa lunging at me.

She hit my hands, sending the pills flying through the air, and the bottle of Jack to the floor.

"What the fuck are you thinking!" she shouted. I had never heard her sound like that.

She knelt on the ground in front of me and brought her hands to my face, trying to get my attention. But all I could concentrate on was the pills that were no longer in my hand and the shards of glass she was undoubtedly kneeling on.

"Leo!" she exclaimed again. "Leo, look at me." She forced my face to hers.

"You promised her!" she shouted, tears rolling down her cheeks.

"One year," I said, blankly.

"Right. One year," she said with a small smile as if she had gotten through to me.

"One year of grieving her."

She nodded.

"I did that," I replied, my eyes finally staring directly into hers, my tone emotionless. "I grieved one year, Teresa. And now I'm done."

I could hear myself saying the words. I knew what I was saying should hurt. I knew talking about suicide—my suicide—should elicit a stronger response. But it didn't. Because I couldn't. In that moment, I was numb.

***

The neighbors had more than likely watched my walk to Teresa's car. Feeling vindicated that they knew I was in there the whole time, defying their demands.

Or maybe they saw me, and like Teresa, pitied me and my appearance. Maybe they closed the curtains that faced my house so they couldn't see me and my overgrown lawn.

I would like to say Teresa's timing was perfect. But perfection would have been an hour later. Maybe two.

However long it takes to die from an overdose.

"When was the last time you left the house?" she asked, her tone low and slightly hoarse.

I shrugged. "A couple weeks? A month? I'm not sure." I didn't look at her. I didn't need to see her expression to know how she felt.

"Where are you taking me?" I asked.

All she kept saying was that it was for Natalie. Maybe we would be visiting her. But that was what I had been trying to do. But instead of visiting, I was trying to stay with her.

"Did you hear me?" she asked.

I glanced at her. Our eyes met briefly. I looked away. "No, sorry."

"She reserved you a room at a detox center."

"You're taking me to rehab?"

"No, a detox center helps you through the withdrawals."

"What's to say I won't go back to drinking after?"

She sighed. "I don't think you're an addict, Leo. You're just grieving."

"How the fuck would you know? I haven't seen you in almost a year."

She nodded. "I've been grieving too."

"Are you checking into the detox center also?" I joked, but it was hollow.

"No, I grieved in other ways."

"I don't have the money to go to a center. And I'm sure my insurance has lapsed."

"Natalie had money put aside for it."

My eyes shot to hers, but she didn't look at me. She stayed stone-faced, looking out the windshield.

"She's sending me to rehab?"

"Detox center," she corrected.

"Whatever. Natalie set this up?"

She nodded.

"And what if I hadn't needed it? What if I hadn't started drinking?"

That's when her eyes met mine. Her eyes told me we all knew there was zero chance of that happening.

"Great. So she knew her husband would become a disgusting piece of shit."

She exhaled and moved her hand to mine. "No, she knew her husband would miss her." She paused, rubbing my hand for a moment and then pulling it away. "However, the two of us miscalculated on how much."

"What do you mean?"

"How long have you been planning that?"

I wish my answer to her on the thought of killing myself was that I had just thought of it that day. Or that I thought of it when Grant left. Or when shit hit the fan with Mark, or her dad, or Christmas. But in all honesty, the plan formed the moment she told me I had a year.

I had spent the year pushing everyone away. A year making sure everyone would have the thought that I was better off dead. That *they* were better off with me dead.

Grant had surprised me. I hadn't expected him to make me feel remotely better.

The job offer was the universe setting me back on track. It was a reminder that everyone's lives would move on, and mine would stay the same.

The plan had been put back into motion.

"Leo, you know that wasn't what she meant by not grieving her after one year."

"Yeah, well she's dead, so she didn't really get a say," I retorted.

Teresa's foot stomped on the brake as she jerked the car to the side of the road.

She whipped off her seatbelt and turned to me, taking my chin and unkempt beard and forcing it toward her like she had done in my room.

"Stop talking like that!" she shouted, both tears and anger in her eyes. "I know she's dead. I know she's not here anymore, Leo. I'm reminded every fucking day of that!"

She let go of my face but kept her eyes on me.

"But you know who *is*? You are, Leo! You're here! And you were about to squander the life that my baby girl didn't get to finish! I know it's hard without her," she continued as the tears broke free. "I know every day you wake up feeling sucker-punched by the realization that she's gone. But you don't get to use her as an excuse to not live!"

"It's not that easy," I said softly, looking away.

"Of course it's not, Leo. Death is the easy part. It's everything that comes after that's hard."

"I've been living in 'hard' for a year. I can't keep doing it."

"Then don't," she exclaimed. "She gave you a year. Your year is up. Go to the detox center. Get clean. Get your head on straight. And then move forward."

I shook my head and ran my hand across my face. "It doesn't work like that, Teresa."

"Well it's going to have to, Leo. Because I made a promise to my daughter. Exactly one year from her death, I was to show up first thing in the morning and drag your ass to a detox center. Then to therapy. I was to parent you, like I would've parented her if you were the one who had died. At least until you're able to look after yourself again."

"Teresa—"

268

"No. You're done talking. You're done making excuses. I will not break the last promise I made to my daughter, and neither will you."

Chapter Fourteen
{Monday, February 25th, 2019}

"Leo, will you come in here please?" my dad asked from the living room the moment I opened the fridge.

I couldn't quite read his tone, but I wasn't one to make him ask something twice.

"What's up?" I asked as I walked from the kitchen. My mom was sitting beside him when I entered the room. "Crap, what'd I do?"

Their faces were serious. Well, my dad's face always was, but I wasn't used to the same unreadable look from my mother.

"Leo, we need to talk," my mom said as she ushered her hand out to the seat in front of them.

We had already had the sex talk. Twice. Well, three times if you counted the brief mention of not wanting grandkids yet that my mom had made the month before.

"Leo," my mom said, pulling me from my daze.

I took a seat. Their demeanor didn't shift. I must have really stepped in it.

"Leo," my mom began, "we want to talk to you about Natalie."

"Dad already gave me the sex talk," I replied as my brows furrowed and my lips curled just slightly on the side.

Her lips stayed pressed in a hard line.

What about Natalie?

"I know, but that's not it," she continued.

"You gotta cut back on seeing Nat," my dad's typically gruff tone sounding harsher with his demand.

"Why?" I asked as I exhaled a laugh.

My mom sighed. "Honey, you two have become really serious really fast."

"Fast? It's been a year."

"Exactly," she said, like she had made her point. Then she sighed. "Leo, you're only seventeen."

"Yeah, I'll be eighteen in three months. Besides, what does age have to do with anything?"

"She's your first girlfriend," she said, trying a new route.

"So? Isn't it good that I found the love of my life on the first try?"

My mom exhaled, looked at my dad, and then looked back at me. "Honey, you don't know what love is. Love isn't what you think it is—it's messy and complicated—"

"I know," I interjected.

"You're too young to know. And your investment in this relationship is unhealthy."

"Unhealthy?" I asked, scrunching my face like I had eaten something sour.

"Honey, we don't even see your friends anymore—" my mom began.

"Yeah, do you even have any?" my dad asked, as my mom backhanded his shoulder.

"It's concerning," she continued. "Natalie has become your whole life. We're just worried about what will happen when you guys break up."

"Wow," I replied, my eyebrows jutting up my forehead. "You seem pretty confident in my relationship's demise."

"Demise?" my dad asked. "You make it seem like a tragedy, kid. You're both in high school. You both live with your parents. Things change. The both of you will too."

"I don't understand. I thought you guys liked Natalie?"

"We do," my mom replied. "She's a wonderful girl. I just want you to be realistic about the likelihood of the two of you ending up together."

"If I say okay, can I go?"

My mom shook her head. "No, I want to really know that you understand."

"Understand what, Mom?" I exclaimed. Dad gave me a look.

I shut my eyes briefly and tried again. "I love Natalie," I said as I stood up. "And I don't know if she'll always love me, but until that day comes, I'm in it."

"In it? Leo, this is your life. This is one girl," my mom said, also getting to her feet.

"She's the girl, Mom."

"Leo, you couldn't possibly know that."

"No? Because I'm too young? What does age have to do with love?"

"The lack of experience," my dad said from his seat.

I shook my head. "So I have to fuck more girls?"

"Leo!" my mom exclaimed.

I should have apologized for my language, but I was on the verge of tears and worried that crying in front of them would only make their point.

"Why would my feelings about Natalie change if I had met other girls before her?"

"Because you would know what you like, what you dislike, what you want out of life—"

"I know what I want," I said. "And it's her. Nothing you say will change that."

"What're you thinking about?" my therapist, Maxwell, asked.

"My parents," I replied.

His brows furrowed. He was used to my lengthy thoughts on Natalie. I mean, she was the reason I was there.

"What about your parents?"

"When they told me there would be other girls. Back when I was first dating Natalie."

"Did you believe them?"

I shook my head as we both laughed. He knew that answer already from the few months he had known me.

"I knew from the very beginning that she was my future." A future no longer available to me. "Those are big feelings to identify at seventeen."

I chuckled. "Yeah, that's what my parents thought too."

"Do you understand their concern now?"

273

I furrowed my brows. "No, I mean, we ended up together. I can't really help if there are other girls after her now. That isn't really by choice."

He nodded. "But look at what came of that love. It may be a little longer than they thought but look at what happened in September. That's what they were scared of. Or some version of that."

He was right. It was why I hadn't told my parents about any of it happening. Not because I couldn't admit they had been right, but because I didn't want them to be scared that I would try it again. As of that moment, I had no intention of that happening.

"I'm sure your parents are thrilled you ended up staying with Natalie. I just want you to see what they saw."

"Why?"

"Because you were seventeen when things got serious for you two." He paused. "When we first met back in September, I started out by asking you to tell me some things about yourself."

I sighed and ran my hand through my hair, trying to think back a few months before. "I honestly don't remember much about that time, Max."

He nodded. "Well, then, good thing I took notes," he replied with a smile. "You said that you and Natalie met when you were sixteen and she was seventeen. That you guys attended the same high school and college. You told me that your favorite color was blue, because that was the color of the dress she was wearing when you knew you were in love with her. You said her favorite music was pop, so that's what you guys always listened to, because you loved to hear her sing to it. And the list goes on like that."

My brows furrowed. Was I in trouble for my answers?

"All of that's true," I stated.

He smiled and nodded. "I guarantee that it is."

"Then what's the problem?"

"Do you see a pattern in it?"

"Not really. You asked me to tell you about me, so I did."

"I heard more about Natalie in that entire thing than I did about you."

"I liked what Natalie liked."

He nodded, but then his expression shifted. "You've been living without Natalie for almost a year and half now. Can you tell me anything about yourself that doesn't involve her?"

I sat silently in my seat, thinking about my life.

"Take your time. It's still early," he added.

In the year after Natalie had died, I had learned I had a high tolerance for alcohol. I learned that calories were calories no matter what form they came in when it came to surviving. I learned not to turn on the car radio, or any radio, because all the stations were preset to her favorite ones, and all the songs reminded me of her.

Months before after I surprisingly had made it out of the detox center, Teresa had picked me up and brought me home. She kept me company. She kept me sane. She helped with the therapy.

"So, what do you got?" Maxwell asked.

"Sorry, I got distracted," I replied.

He laughed. "I wouldn't be a good therapist if I didn't know my client well enough to know when he's daydreaming."

I smiled. "True."

"So, what have you learned about yourself?"

"Well, I don't like to cook, but I've known that for a long time. Not just that I don't like it. I genuinely suck at it."

He smiled and nodded.

"I like classic rock—AC/DC in particular."

"Any certain reason?"

"It's not sappy, and it doesn't remind me of Nat."

He smiled and nodded once more.

"And I still like the color blue. Not just because she looked stunning in that dress, but also because it's just a nice color."

"That's all a great start."

"Yeah?"

"Absolutely. Leo, you built an entire life with someone else. Your interests and likes were bound to overlap. I just want you to start processing which parts of that life were *you* and which ones were *her*. Learning who you are will help you move forward. Maybe someday meet someone."

"I don't think I'm quite ready for that yet."

"And that's okay. There's no set timeline to any of this. It's all at your own pace."

"Diane set me up on a blind date. Although she didn't call it a date. She said it was a business meeting, even though I have yet to be back to work."

"How did it go?"

"Terrible," I said with a laugh. "I mean, the woman was beautiful and funny, but I don't know, it didn't feel right."

"Because of Natalie?"

"No," I immediately corrected. "I mean, at first it felt a little weird because of her, but then, I don't know, I just didn't feel *it*."

He nodded. He was married. He more than likely understood.

"And as long as you're open to feeling *it* again, then we've made progress."

I smiled. I hoped that was true.

I felt like I had made progress over the past few months.

I hadn't quit drinking, but I wasn't knocking back fifths anymore. Actually, I was staying away from whiskey all together. I had sold my house after the new year. My thirty days to leave were almost up. I wasn't sure what was going to come from that yet—pain or relief.

Teresa had stayed with me like she promised Natalie. It gave us time to catch up. Gave us time to talk about Natalie. Gave us time to say good-bye before we went our separate ways.

"So, how are you sleeping? Are the edibles helping?" Maxwell asked as he finished typing some notes.

"Yeah. I don't remember the last time I slept a full night. Even before Nat died, I was so anxious about everything, I wasn't sleeping then either."

"Well, I'm glad they helped." He paused, then began again. "Do you think you're ready to go back to work?"

I exhaled and ran my hand through my hair. "Actually, I went in and talked to Wayne last week."

He leaned back in his chair. "Oh, really? How'd it go?"

I chuckled. "Way better than it should've. Especially after I ignored his phone calls for most of last year," I replied, shaking my head. "I swear that man's a saint."

"Or maybe he's just been in your shoes, like you said."

"I guess," I replied with a shrug. "But to not only hold my job for me all this time, but to say he understood when I said I wasn't coming back—"

"You're not going back?"

I glanced up at Maxwell. "I decided not to," I replied, not knowing what that said about my progress.

"Why not?"

"A few reasons," I responded with a sigh. "But the main one being I just don't feel like that's me anymore."

"What do you mean?"

"I don't know how to describe it exactly. It's like the moment I met Natalie, I felt like an adult. Because I was in love. I had this need to take care of her. To be with her. We graduated, and I knew I needed to get a good job. I didn't really know what I wanted to do, but I knew what I was good at, so I went to school for that. I got a job so we could plan a wedding. I took the promotions so we could have more money. I did everything to advance the life we wanted together."

"Lots of Natalie in that."

278

"Exactly."

"I'm glad to see you identified that yourself."

"So it's not bad that I'm jobless?"

"Well, I mean, it makes paying bills hard, but just because you don't want *that* job doesn't mean you can't get another one."

I nodded. "The sale for my house is all finalized. I got the check this morning."

"That's great. Have you found a new place?"

I nodded. "And I got an apartment this time, because I could actually have some time to not work. But this time, instead of drinking, I was thinking I would get to know myself—without Nat."

"I think that's a great idea."

"I'm glad," I replied with an exhale. "I was worried you would think this was a step back. Like I was running from things instead of dealing with it."

He shook his head. "Leo, I wouldn't qualify this as running."

"Even if I'm moving to Studio City?"

He raised his brows. "That's a big change."

"Still think I'm not running?"

"No, still not running," he replied with a laugh. "But it is a big step. How do you feel?"

"Nervous."

He nodded.

"It feels like how I should've felt when I left my parents for college."

"You weren't nervous then?"

I shook my head. "No, I was moving on campus, and Natalie was going to be closer, and there was going to be no parents."

He laughed. "Ah, makes sense."

"Yeah, so this is my first official on my own. No parents. No brother. No Natalie."

"What about last year in your house?"

"I don't know if that counts with how intoxicated I was the entire time."

"Yeah, I can see how the nerves wouldn't be as big."

We laughed.

"So, in general, how are you feeling?"

I shrugged. "Healthy."

"That's a great description. You look healthy."

I nodded, giving him a grin.

"Any other descriptive words?"

"Uh—I don't know. Is 'fine' okay? It doesn't seem very descriptive."

"It's not, but it is fine to use," he joked.

"Well, then, fine it is."

"Perfect. Well, I want you to keep working on finding those descriptive words. As you progress, think about what you are. Maybe next you'll be *okay*. Then content. Maybe eventually even happy."

"That would be great."

"I assume by the move I won't be seeing you anymore."

"Yeah, that would be correct."

He gave a half-hearted smile. "The work doesn't stop here, ya know. You became someone's other half before you were even a whole. It's important that you work on finding out who you are. If you don't, you risk never really getting to know the real you. The Leo outside of love and relationships."

***

The boxes were all packed. Not that there were many. The only things I hadn't pawned were things with sentimental value.

Teresa took some stuff I didn't want to donate but couldn't bring it with me. Maxwell reminded me that leaving was a fresh start. He reminded me that Natalie wasn't going with me. But I could take something to remember her by.

A photo from our honeymoon slipped from the top of a box as I loaded it into the back of the truck and floated to the ground.

"How do you feel?" Natalie asked from the passenger seat of our car.

"What do you mean?" I asked with a chuckle. "I feel fine."

I put on my blinker, preparing to enter the highway as we began our drive.

"No, I mean, now that you're a husband."

"I feel the same—I mean I've felt like your husband for a while now."

She smiled and shook her head as if to disagree with me.

"Why? Do you feel different?" I asked.

She exhaled, but not out of frustration. "I do. I don't know what it is—I just feel—older, maybe?"

"I didn't want to say anything, but I definitely noticed that you had aged seemingly overnight."

She playfully hit my arm, while we both laughed. "Ass," she said. "I mean, I feel like it's a whole new beginning."

I shut the back of the moving truck and walked back into the house.

Diane was there, doing what Diane always did, checking to make sure everything was completed. When I walked into the kitchen, she glanced over and smiled. I was glad she didn't hate me. I would hate me after how I had treated her for the past year.

"All packed up?" she asked.

"Yeah. But I'm not really sure why I rented an entire truck."

"Yeah, what happened to all your stuff?"

"I downsized."

She nodded and walked over to the box on the kitchen counter of things she was taking with her.

"Want to grab breakfast before you take off?"

"I told the apartment manager I would pick up the keys by noon."

She nodded.

"Rain check?"

"Of course."

She went to pick up her box, but I moved past her and grabbed it instead.

"Thanks," she said, walking behind me to her car. "So any particular reason you chose Studio City?" she asked.

I set the box on her back seat, shut the door, and then shrugged. "I found an apartment that wasn't outrageously priced."

She smiled. "Was that your only criteria?"

"That and it was close to a lot of take-out places."

"Ah, that makes much more sense."

She looked down at her hands, as I ran my hand through my hair.

"Look, ah—you've been a—"

"Yeah, you too," she interjected, knowing what I was struggling to get out.

And she *had* been a great friend. Not only to Natalie, but to me.

"I wanted to thank you for everything you've done for me this last year—"

"No need. I was just doing my job."

"Just because you're a lawyer doesn't mean you have to clean up my mess."

She shook her head. "I didn't mean my job as a lawyer. I meant my job as your friend."

I smiled, as she reciprocated with one of her own. Before I could say anything else, she threw her arms around me, and I pulled her tightly to my chest.

"Please be good to my friend," she whispered into my ear. "He's a good man."

Tears lingered in my eyes, as I kissed her cheek, and pulled away. She used her thumb to wipe a tear that had escaped.

"I'll see you around?" I asked.

"You do know Studio City is only like thirty minutes away, right?"

I laughed. "Yeah, well, we all know proximity has little to do with people staying in touch."

She nodded. "Well, you know who to call whenever you need a lawyer."

I shook my head and smirked, glancing down before my eyes met hers one more time. "Thanks for everything, Diane."

She got in her car and pulled away.

Thirty minutes or not, things would be so different. I was bound and determined to do what Maxwell said and immerse myself in my new life. I was hell-bent on making sure I didn't let Teresa down by wasting the life Natalie didn't get.

The thought of her still hit hard, but it was easier to see the light at the end of the tunnel when not drowning in the depressant.

I waited until Diane's car was out of sight and walked back into the house, grabbing the last of my things off the counter. My eyes shut as I took a minute to remember the life I had built there—the life *we* had built. My wife was gone, but not forgotten, and the man she had married had been buried with her.

I didn't just *want* to be someone different but *needed* to be. If I felt different, moving on would be easier. And I promised her I would. Well, I made her a lot of promises I hadn't intended on keeping. But I was on the other side of that lapse in judgment now, and I was bound and determined to not let it lapse again.

Natalie's eyes could barely stay open. Her voice was frail and her breaths shallow. Everything inside of me ached, wishing I could take away her pain. I knew that dying would do that, but I wasn't ready for her to be gone.

I shut my eyes as a tear streamed down my cheek.

"Leo," Natalie said softly.

I opened my eyes, staring into hers.

"What do you need?" I asked, prepared to wet her lips, or administer medication.

"Be happy," she stated, before her eyes shut again.

I thought that was all I was going to get, but then her eyes opened again. She was fighting it.

"I want you—to be happy," she began again. "You have your— whole life—still."

"You're my life," I replied, stroking her brittle hair.

She shook her head slightly. "Not any—more."

My brows furrowed. She wasn't even gone yet, and she was saying she was no longer my life.

"Nat—"

"Be happy—" she said for the third time. "Love again." She shifted just slightly in the bed as her eyelids closed. "Love them like—you loved me."

The End

About the Author

Jennifer R. Jensen is a fiction author who dove back into the world of writing in 2019. She had spent a decade away from her passion becoming a wife, mom, and advancing her career. With six independently published books and two novellas under her belt, she is beginning to expand her love and knowledge for writing into the world of traditional publishing. She is looking forward to the next big adventure in her writing career that will expand her knowledge on the publishing process and take her creative works to the next level.

For more information on her books go to
WWW.JenniferJensenBooks.com

Made in the USA
Middletown, DE
22 October 2023

41240696R00172